GOSCINNY AND UDERZO
PRESENT
An Asterix Adventure

ASTERIX
IN
CORSICA

Written by RENÉ GOSCINNY *and Illustrated by* ALBERT UDERZO

Translated by Anthea Bell *and* Derek Hockridge

Orion
Children's Books

Asterix titles available now

1 Asterix the Gaul
2 Asterix and the Golden Sickle
3 Asterix and the Goths
4 Asterix the Gladiator
5 Asterix and the Banquet
6 Asterix and Cleopatra
7 Asterix and the Big Fight
8 Asterix in Britain
9 Asterix and the Normans
10 Asterix the Legionary
11 Asterix and the Chieftain's Shield
12 Asterix at the Olympic Games
13 Asterix and the Cauldron
14 Asterix in Spain
15 Asterix and the Roman Agent
16 Asterix in Switzerland
17 The Mansions of the Gods
18 Asterix and the Laurel Wreath
19 Asterix and the Soothsayer
20 Asterix in Corsica
21 Asterix and Caesar's Gift
22 Asterix and the Great Crossing
23 Obelix and Co.
24 Asterix in Belgium
25 Asterix and the Great Divide
26 Asterix and the Black Gold
27 Asterix and Son
28 Asterix and the Magic Carpet
29 Asterix and the Secret Weapon
30 Asterix and Obelix All at Sea
31 Asterix and the Actress
32 Asterix and the Class Act
33 Asterix and the Falling Sky
34 Asterix and Obelix's Birthday – the Golden Book
35 Asterix and the Picts
36 Asterix and the Missing Scroll

Where's Asterix?
Where's Dogmatix?
Asterix and the Vikings
Asterix at the Olympic Games (film tie-in)
How Obelix Fell into the Magic Potion
Asterix Omnibus 1 (Books 1-3)
Asterix Omnibus 2 (Books 4-6)
Asterix Omnibus 3 (Books 7-9)
Asterix Omnibus 4 (Books 10-12)
Asterix Omnibus 5 (Books 13-15)
Asterix Omnibus 6 (Books 16-18)
Asterix Omnibus 7 (Books 19-21)
Asterix Omnibus 8 (Books 22-24)
Asterix Omnibus 9 (Books 25-27)
Asterix Omnibus 10 (Books 28-30)
Asterix Omnibus 11 (Books 31-33)

ORION CHILDREN'S BOOKS

This revised edition first published in 2004 by Orion Books Ltd
This edition published in 2016 by Hodder and Stoughton

1 3 5 7 9 10 8 6 4 2

Original title: *Astérix en Corse*
Exclusive licensee: Hachette Children's Group
Translators: Anthea Bell and Derek Hockridge
Typography: Bryony Newhouse

A CIP record for this book is available from the British Library

ISBN 978-0-7528-6643-7 (cased)
ISBN 978-0-7528-6644-4 (paperback)
ISBN 978-1-4440-1327-6 (ebook)

Printed in China

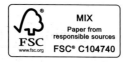

MIX
Paper from responsible sources
FSC® C104740

Orion Children's Books
An imprint of Hachette Children's Group, part of Hodder and Stoughton
Carmelite House, 50 Victoria Embankment
London EC4Y 0DZ
An Hachette UK Company

www.hachette.co.uk
www.asterix.com
www.hachettechildrens.co.uk

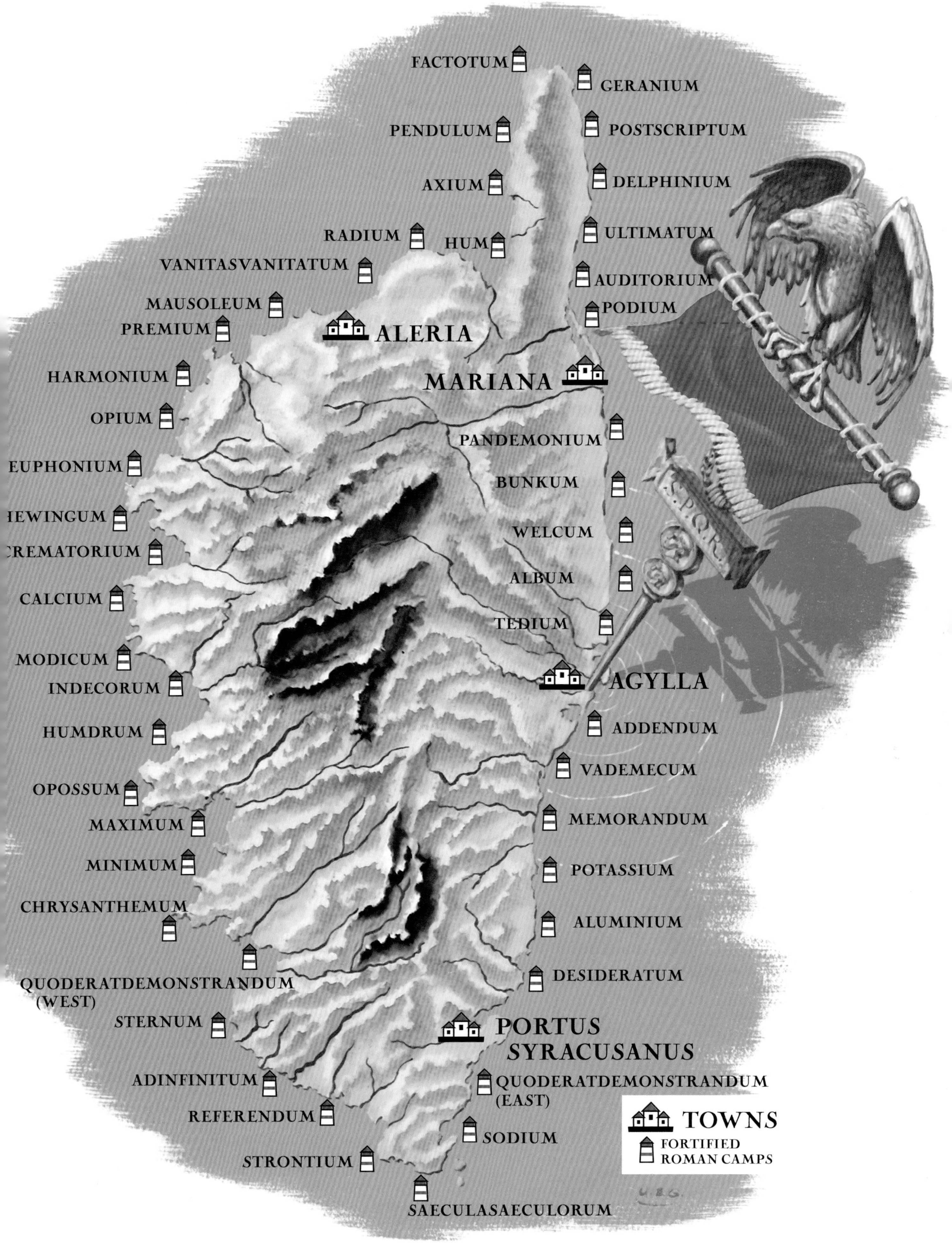
FACTOTUM
GERANIUM
PENDULUM
POSTSCRIPTUM
AXIUM
DELPHINIUM
RADIUM
HUM
ULTIMATUM
VANITASVANITATUM
AUDITORIUM
MAUSOLEUM
PODIUM
PREMIUM
ALERIA
HARMONIUM
MARIANA
OPIUM
PANDEMONIUM
EUPHONIUM
BUNKUM
EWINGUM
WELCUM
REMATORIUM
ALBUM
CALCIUM
TEDIUM
MODICUM
AGYLLA
INDECORUM
ADDENDUM
HUMDRUM
VADEMECUM
OPOSSUM
MAXIMUM
MEMORANDUM
MINIMUM
POTASSIUM
CHRYSANTHEMUM
ALUMINIUM
QUODERATDEMONSTRANDUM
(WEST)
DESIDERATUM
STERNUM
PORTUS
SYRACUSANUS
ADINFINITUM
QUODERATDEMONSTRANDUM
(EAST)
REFERENDUM
TOWNS
SODIUM
FORTIFIED
ROMAN CAMPS
STRONTIUM
SAECULASAECULORUM

PREAMBLE

For most people, Corsica is the homeland of an emperor who has left pages in history as indelible as those inspired by our old friend Julius Caesar. It is also the birthplace of Tino Rossi, a singer with a long and prestigious career whose songs about Marinella and Bella Catarineta have toured the world. It is a country of vendettas, siestas, complicated political games, strong cheeses, wild pigs, chestnuts, succulent blackbirds, and spry old men watching the world go by.

But Corsica is more than all that. It is one of those privileged places in the world with a character, a strong personality that neither time nor man has ever tamed. It is one of the most beautiful places in the world – no wonder people call it the Isle of Beauty.

But why this preamble, you may ask. Because the Corsicans, who are described as individualists – having both exuberance and self-control – nonchalant, hospitable, loyal, faithful in friendship, attached to their homeland, eloquent and courageous, are also more than all that.

They are sensitive.

The Authors

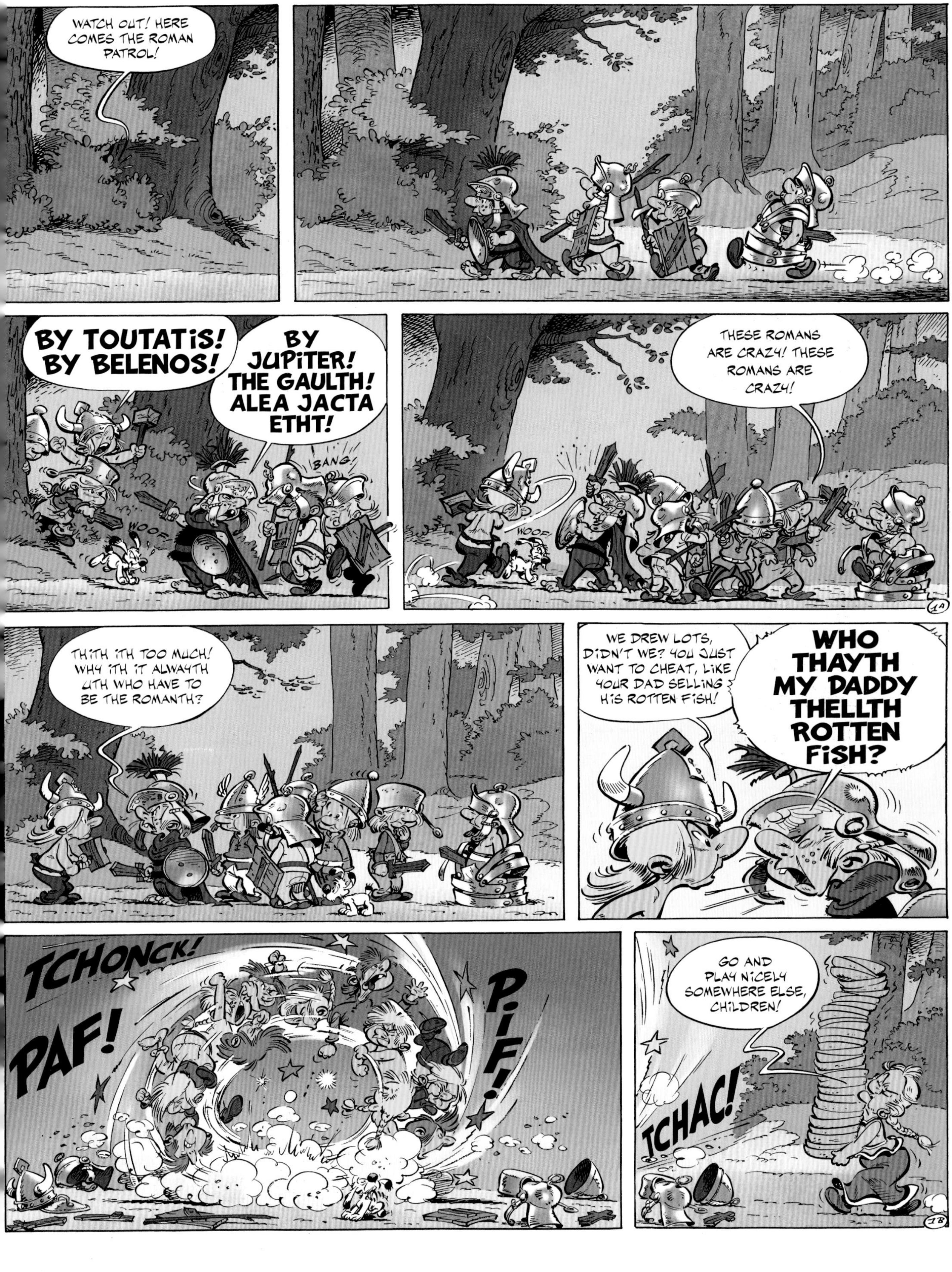
WATCH OUT! HERE COMES THE ROMAN PATROL!
BY TOUTATIS! BY BELENOS!
BY JUPITER! THE GAULTH! ALEA JACTA ETHT!
BANG!
WOOF!
THESE ROMANS ARE CRAZY! THESE ROMANS ARE CRAZY!
WOOF!
THITH ITH TOO MUCH! WHY ITH IT ALWAYTH UTH WHO HAVE TO BE THE ROMANTH?
WE DREW LOTS, DIDN'T WE? YOU JUST WANT TO CHEAT, LIKE YOUR DAD SELLING HIS ROTTEN FISH!
WHO THAYTH MY DADDY THELLTH ROTTEN FISH?
TCHONCK!
PAF!
PIF!
GO AND PLAY NICELY SOMEWHERE ELSE, CHILDREN!
TCHAC!

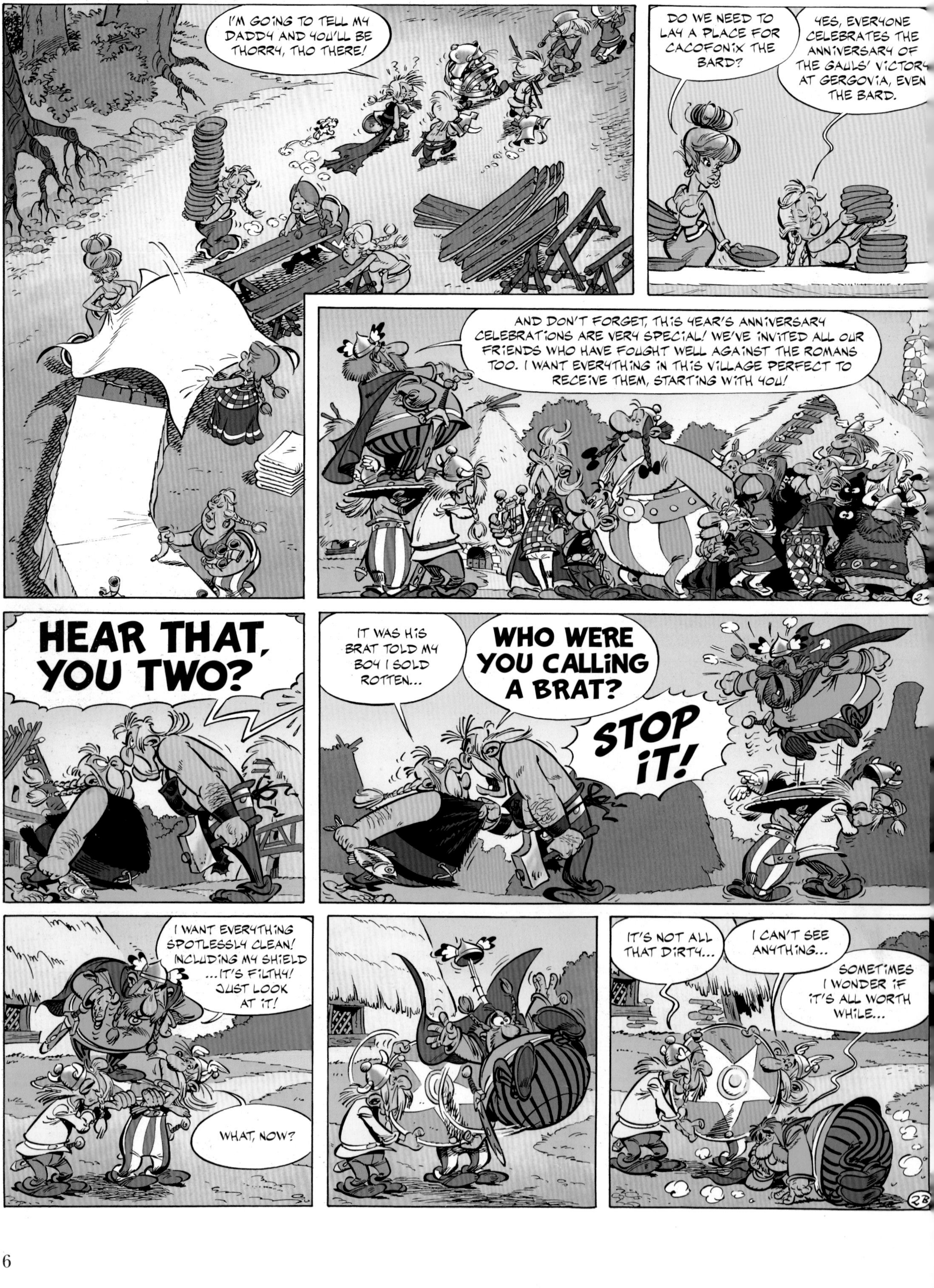
I'M GOING TO TELL MY DADDY AND YOU'LL BE THORRY, THO THERE!
DO WE NEED TO LAY A PLACE FOR CACOFONIX THE BARD?
YES, EVERYONE CELEBRATES THE ANNIVERSARY OF THE GAULS' VICTORY AT GERGOVIA, EVEN THE BARD.
AND DON'T FORGET, THIS YEAR'S ANNIVERSARY CELEBRATIONS ARE VERY SPECIAL! WE'VE INVITED ALL OUR FRIENDS WHO HAVE FOUGHT WELL AGAINST THE ROMANS TOO. I WANT EVERYTHING IN THIS VILLAGE PERFECT TO RECEIVE THEM, STARTING WITH YOU!
HEAR THAT, YOU TWO?
IT WAS HIS BRAT TOLD MY BOY I SOLD ROTTEN...
WHO WERE YOU CALLING A BRAT?
STOP IT!
I WANT EVERYTHING SPOTLESSLY CLEAN! INCLUDING MY SHIELD ...IT'S FILTHY! JUST LOOK AT IT!
WHAT, NOW?
IT'S NOT ALL THAT DIRTY...
I CAN'T SEE ANYTHING...
SOMETIMES I WONDER IF IT'S ALL WORTH WHILE...

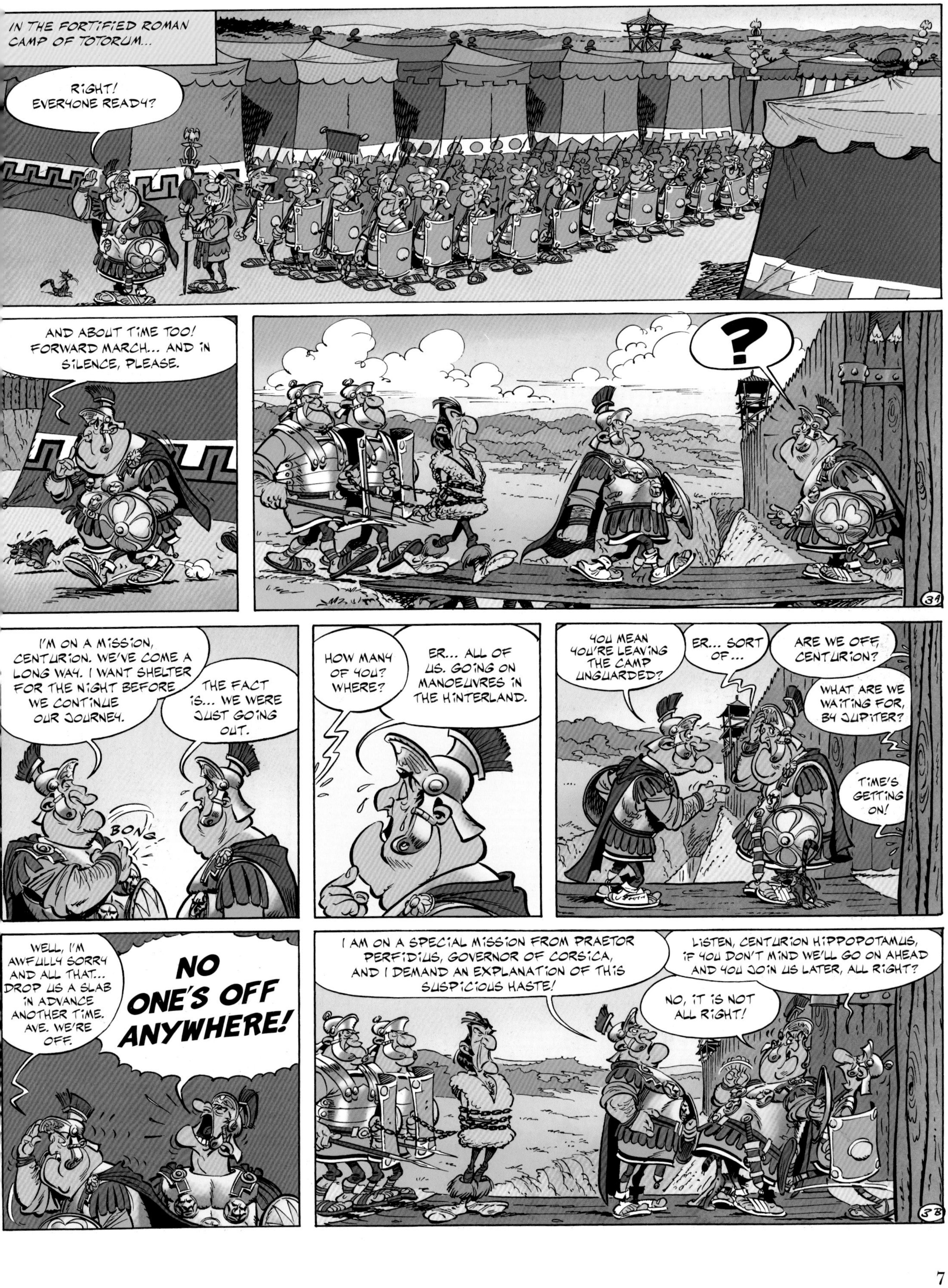
IN THE FORTIFIED ROMAN CAMP OF TOTORUM...
RIGHT! EVERYONE READY?
AND ABOUT TIME TOO! FORWARD MARCH... AND IN SILENCE, PLEASE.
?
I'M ON A MISSION, CENTURION. WE'VE COME A LONG WAY. I WANT SHELTER FOR THE NIGHT BEFORE WE CONTINUE OUR JOURNEY.
THE FACT IS... WE WERE JUST GOING OUT.
BONG!
HOW MANY OF YOU? WHERE?
ER... ALL OF US. GOING ON MANOEUVRES IN THE HINTERLAND.
YOU MEAN YOU'RE LEAVING THE CAMP UNGUARDED?
ER... SORT OF...
ARE WE OFF, CENTURION?
WHAT ARE WE WAITING FOR, BY JUPITER?
TIME'S GETTING ON!
WELL, I'M AWFULLY SORRY AND ALL THAT... DROP US A SLAB IN ADVANCE ANOTHER TIME. AVE. WE'RE OFF.
NO ONE'S OFF ANYWHERE!
I AM ON A SPECIAL MISSION FROM PRAETOR PERFIDIUS, GOVERNOR OF CORSICA, AND I DEMAND AN EXPLANATION OF THIS SUSPICIOUS HASTE!
LISTEN, CENTURION HIPPOPOTAMUS, IF YOU DON'T MIND WE'LL GO ON AHEAD AND YOU JOIN US LATER, ALL RIGHT?
NO, IT IS NOT ALL RIGHT!

HERE, COME INTO MY TENT... DON'T START WITHOUT ME, YOU LOT. THIS WON'T TAKE LONG.

?

TODAY IS THE ANNIVERSARY OF THE BATTLE OF GERGOVIA. THE PEOPLE OF THE NEARBY GAULISH VILLAGE HAVE A WAY OF CELEBRATING THE OCCASION BY ATTACKING THE NEIGHBOURING ROMAN GARRISONS.

AND YOU DON'T ATTEMPT TO STOP THIS LOCAL CUSTOM?

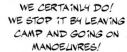

WE CERTAINLY DO! WE STOP IT BY LEAVING CAMP AND GOING ON MANOEUVRES!

ARE YOU READY, CENTURION HIPPOPOTAMUS? THE BOYS ARE GETTING A BIT IMPATIENT, AND...

ARE THESE GAULS REALLY SO FEROCIOUS?

WELL, TOO BAD. I'M ESCORTING A CORSICAN EXILE, AND HE'S SPENDING THE NIGHT IN THIS CAMP. YOU AND YOUR GARRISON ARE RESPONSIBLE TO CAESAR FOR HIS SAFE KEEPING. I'LL BE BACK TO PICK HIM UP TOMORROW.

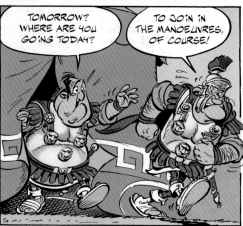

TOMORROW? WHERE ARE YOU GOING TODAY?

TO JOIN IN THE MANOEUVRES, OF COURSE!

BUT... BUT YOU CAN'T DO THIS TO US! THE GAULS WILL SLAUGHTER US! WHAT'S MORE, IF THEY SEE WE'VE GOT A PRISONER HERE, THEY'LL...

BRING THE EXILE ALONG!

AVE, CENTURION, AND DON'T FORGET, CAESAR WILL HOLD YOU RESPONSIBLE!

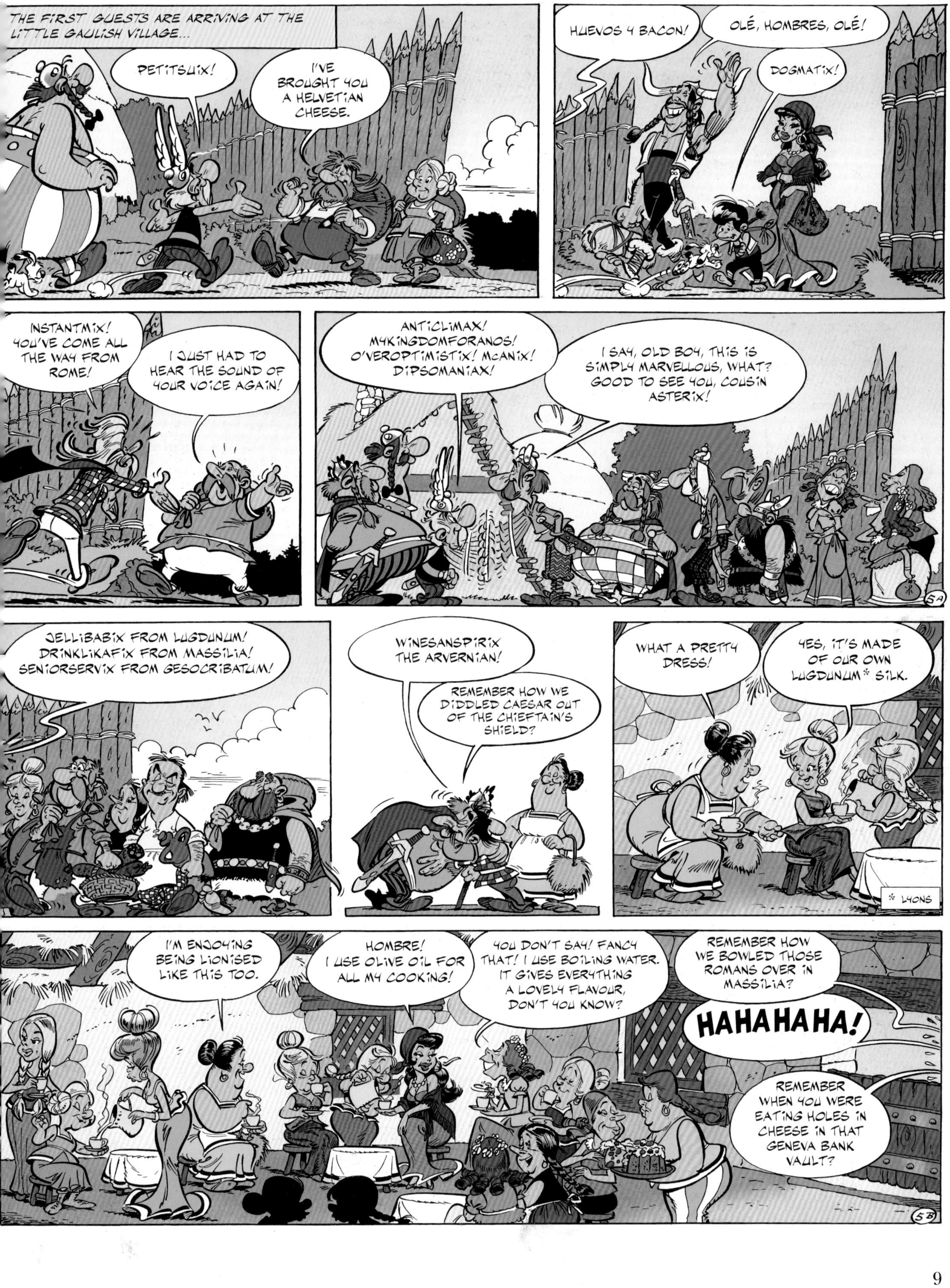
THE FIRST GUESTS ARE ARRIVING AT THE LITTLE GAULISH VILLAGE...
PETITSUIX!
I'VE BROUGHT YOU A HELVETIAN CHEESE.
HUEVOS Y BACON!
OLÉ, HOMBRES, OLÉ!
DOGMATIX!
INSTANTMIX! YOU'VE COME ALL THE WAY FROM ROME!
I JUST HAD TO HEAR THE SOUND OF YOUR VOICE AGAIN!
ANTICLIMAX! MYKINGDOMFORANOS! O'VEROPTIMISTIX! McANIX! DIPSOMANIAX!
I SAY, OLD BOY, THIS IS SIMPLY MARVELLOUS, WHAT? GOOD TO SEE YOU, COUSIN ASTERIX!
JELLIBABIX FROM LUGDUNUM! DRINKLIKAFIX FROM MASSILIA! SENIORSERVIX FROM GESOCRIBATUM!
WINESANSPIRIX THE ARVERNIAN!
REMEMBER HOW WE DIDDLED CAESAR OUT OF THE CHIEFTAIN'S SHIELD?
WHAT A PRETTY DRESS!
YES, IT'S MADE OF OUR OWN LUGDUNUM* SILK.
* LYONS
I'M ENJOYING BEING LIONISED LIKE THIS TOO.
HOMBRE! I USE OLIVE OIL FOR ALL MY COOKING!
YOU DON'T SAY! FANCY THAT! I USE BOILING WATER. IT GIVES EVERYTHING A LOVELY FLAVOUR, DON'T YOU KNOW?
REMEMBER HOW WE BOWLED THOSE ROMANS OVER IN MASSILIA?
HAHAHAHA!
REMEMBER WHEN YOU WERE EATING HOLES IN CHEESE IN THAT GENEVA BANK VAULT?

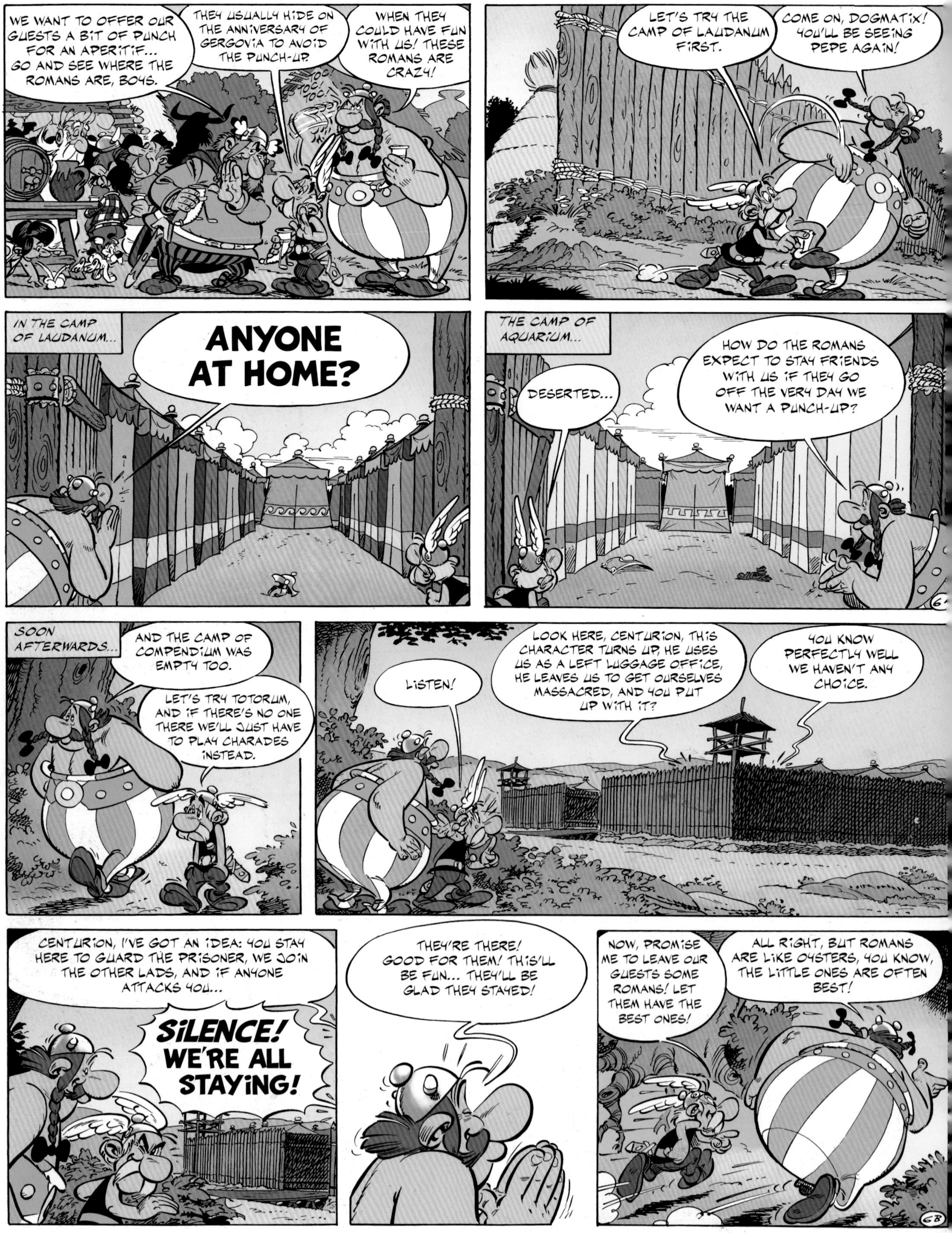

WE WANT TO OFFER OUR GUESTS A BIT OF PUNCH FOR AN APERITIF... GO AND SEE WHERE THE ROMANS ARE, BOYS.
THEY USUALLY HIDE ON THE ANNIVERSARY OF GERGOVIA TO AVOID THE PUNCH-UP.
WHEN THEY COULD HAVE FUN WITH US! THESE ROMANS ARE CRAZY!
LET'S TRY THE CAMP OF LAUDANUM FIRST.
COME ON, DOGMATIX! YOU'LL BE SEEING PEPE AGAIN!
IN THE CAMP OF LAUDANUM...
ANYONE AT HOME?
THE CAMP OF AQUARIUM...
DESERTED...
HOW DO THE ROMANS EXPECT TO STAY FRIENDS WITH US IF THEY GO OFF THE VERY DAY WE WANT A PUNCH-UP?
SOON AFTERWARDS...
AND THE CAMP OF COMPENDIUM WAS EMPTY TOO.
LET'S TRY TOTORUM, AND IF THERE'S NO ONE THERE WE'LL JUST HAVE TO PLAY CHARADES INSTEAD.
LISTEN!
LOOK HERE, CENTURION, THIS CHARACTER TURNS UP, HE USES US AS A LEFT LUGGAGE OFFICE, HE LEAVES US TO GET OURSELVES MASSACRED, AND YOU PUT UP WITH IT?
YOU KNOW PERFECTLY WELL WE HAVEN'T ANY CHOICE.
CENTURION, I'VE GOT AN IDEA: YOU STAY HERE TO GUARD THE PRISONER, WE JOIN THE OTHER LADS, AND IF ANYONE ATTACKS YOU...
SILENCE! WE'RE ALL STAYING!
THEY'RE THERE! GOOD FOR THEM! THIS'LL BE FUN... THEY'LL BE GLAD THEY STAYED!
NOW, PROMISE ME TO LEAVE OUR GUESTS SOME ROMANS! LET THEM HAVE THE BEST ONES!
ALL RIGHT, BUT ROMANS ARE LIKE OYSTERS, YOU KNOW, THE LITTLE ONES ARE OFTEN BEST!

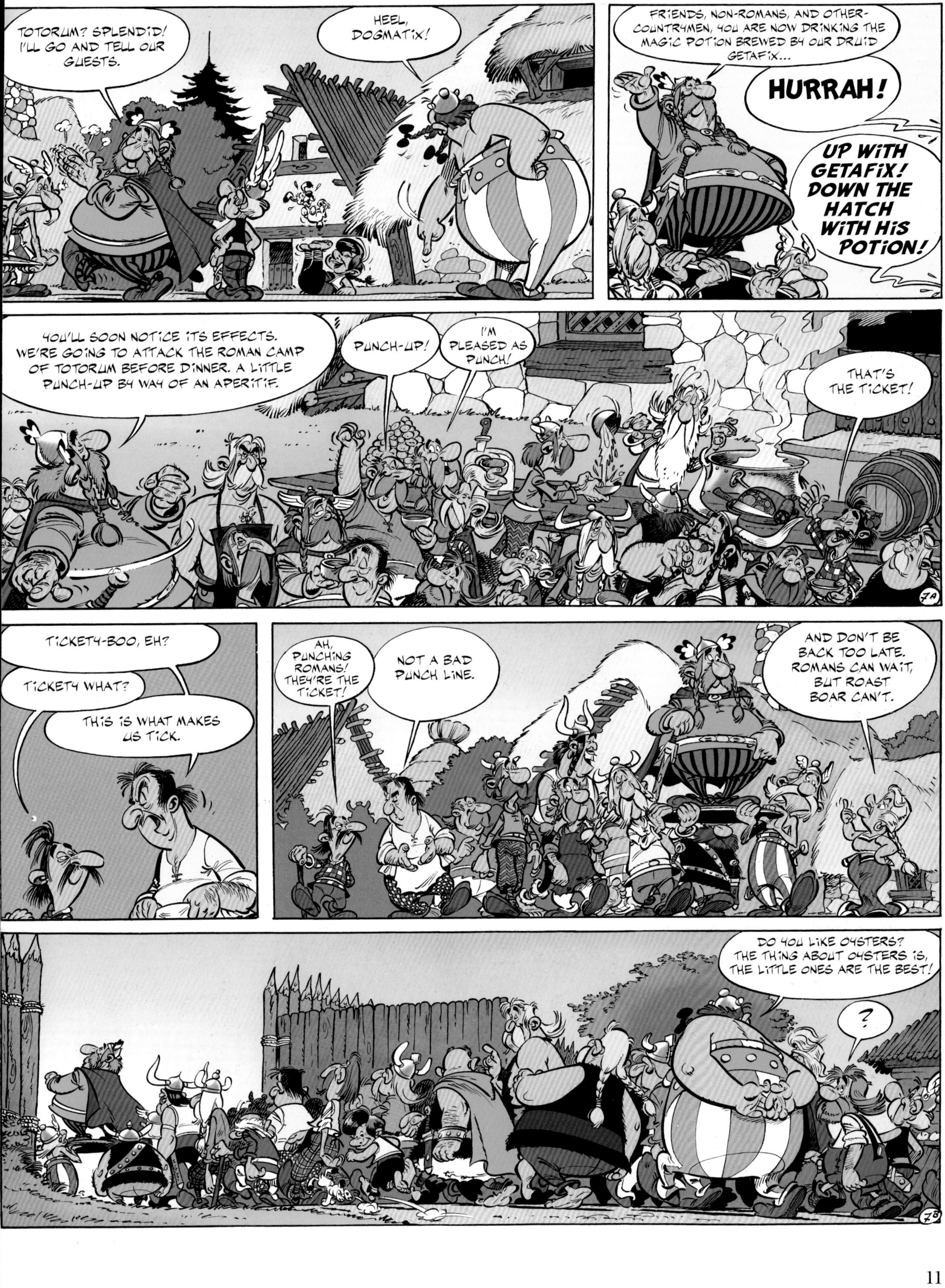
TOTORUM? SPLENDID! I'LL GO AND TELL OUR GUESTS.
HEEL, DOGMATIX!
FRIENDS, NON-ROMANS, AND OTHER-COUNTRYMEN, YOU ARE NOW DRINKING THE MAGIC POTION BREWED BY OUR DRUID GETAFIX...
HURRAH!
UP WITH GETAFIX! DOWN THE HATCH WITH HIS POTION!
YOU'LL SOON NOTICE ITS EFFECTS. WE'RE GOING TO ATTACK THE ROMAN CAMP OF TOTORUM BEFORE DINNER. A LITTLE PUNCH-UP BY WAY OF AN APERITIF.
PUNCH-UP!
I'M PLEASED AS PUNCH!
THAT'S THE TICKET!
7A
TICKETY-BOO, EH?
TICKETY WHAT?
THIS IS WHAT MAKES US TICK.
AH, PUNCHING ROMANS! THEY'RE THE TICKET!
NOT A BAD PUNCH LINE.
AND DON'T BE BACK TOO LATE. ROMANS CAN WAIT, BUT ROAST BOAR CAN'T.
DO YOU LIKE OYSTERS? THE THING ABOUT OYSTERS IS, THE LITTLE ONES ARE THE BEST!
?
7B

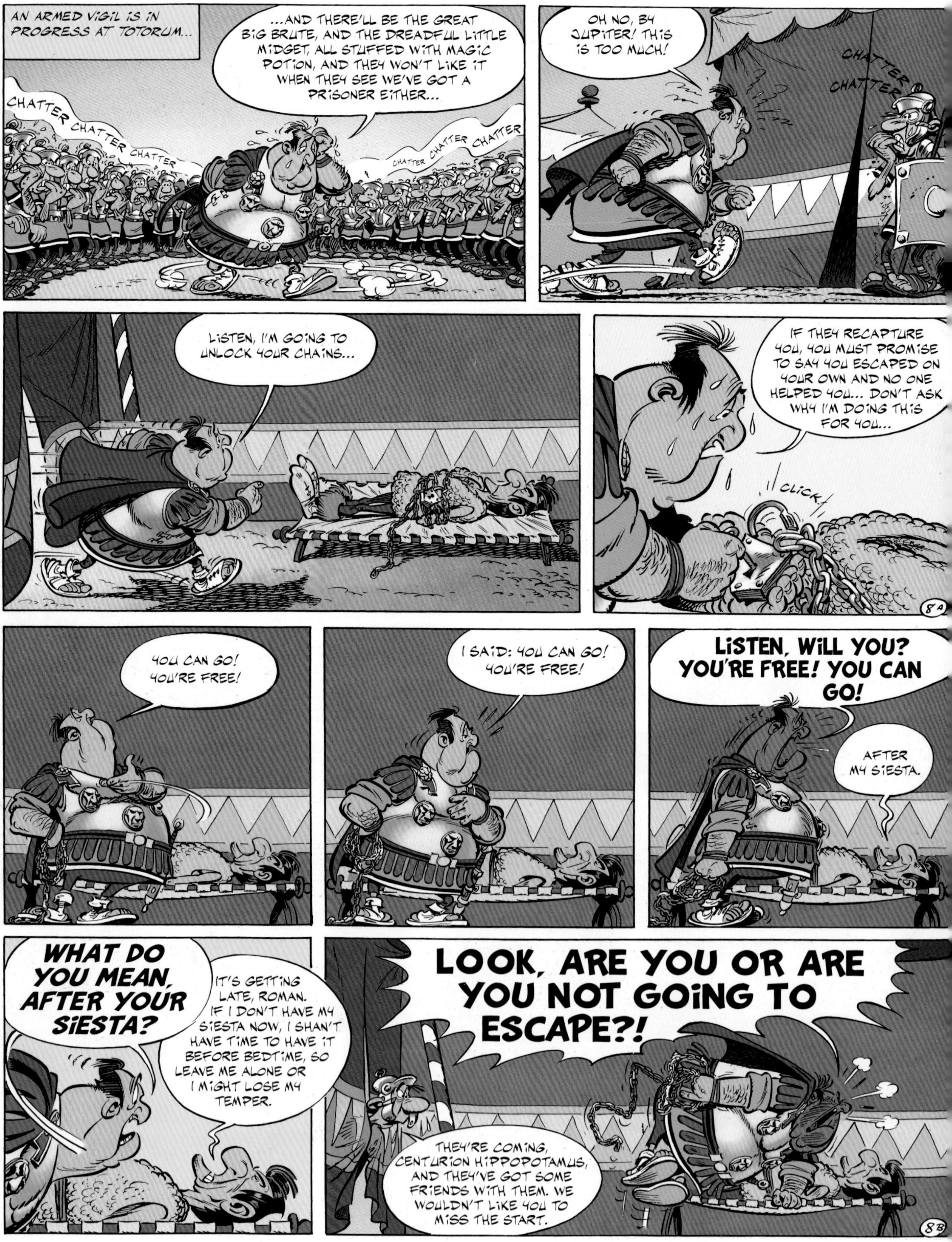
AN ARMED VIGIL IS IN PROGRESS AT TOTORUM...
...AND THERE'LL BE THE GREAT BIG BRUTE, AND THE DREADFUL LITTLE MIDGET, ALL STUFFED WITH MAGIC POTION, AND THEY WON'T LIKE IT WHEN THEY SEE WE'VE GOT A PRISONER EITHER...
CHATTER CHATTER CHATTER
CHATTER CHATTER CHATTER
OH NO, BY JUPITER! THIS IS TOO MUCH!
CHATTER CHATTER
LISTEN, I'M GOING TO UNLOCK YOUR CHAINS...
IF THEY RECAPTURE YOU, YOU MUST PROMISE TO SAY YOU ESCAPED ON YOUR OWN AND NO ONE HELPED YOU... DON'T ASK WHY I'M DOING THIS FOR YOU...
CLICK
8A
YOU CAN GO! YOU'RE FREE!
I SAID: YOU CAN GO! YOU'RE FREE!
LISTEN, WILL YOU? YOU'RE FREE! YOU CAN GO!
AFTER MY SIESTA.
WHAT DO YOU MEAN, AFTER YOUR SIESTA?
IT'S GETTING LATE, ROMAN. IF I DON'T HAVE MY SIESTA NOW, I SHAN'T HAVE TIME TO HAVE IT BEFORE BEDTIME, SO LEAVE ME ALONE OR I MIGHT LOSE MY TEMPER.
LOOK, ARE YOU OR ARE YOU NOT GOING TO ESCAPE?!
THEY'RE COMING, CENTURION HIPPOPOTAMUS, AND THEY'VE GOT SOME FRIENDS WITH THEM. WE WOULDN'T LIKE YOU TO MISS THE START.
8B

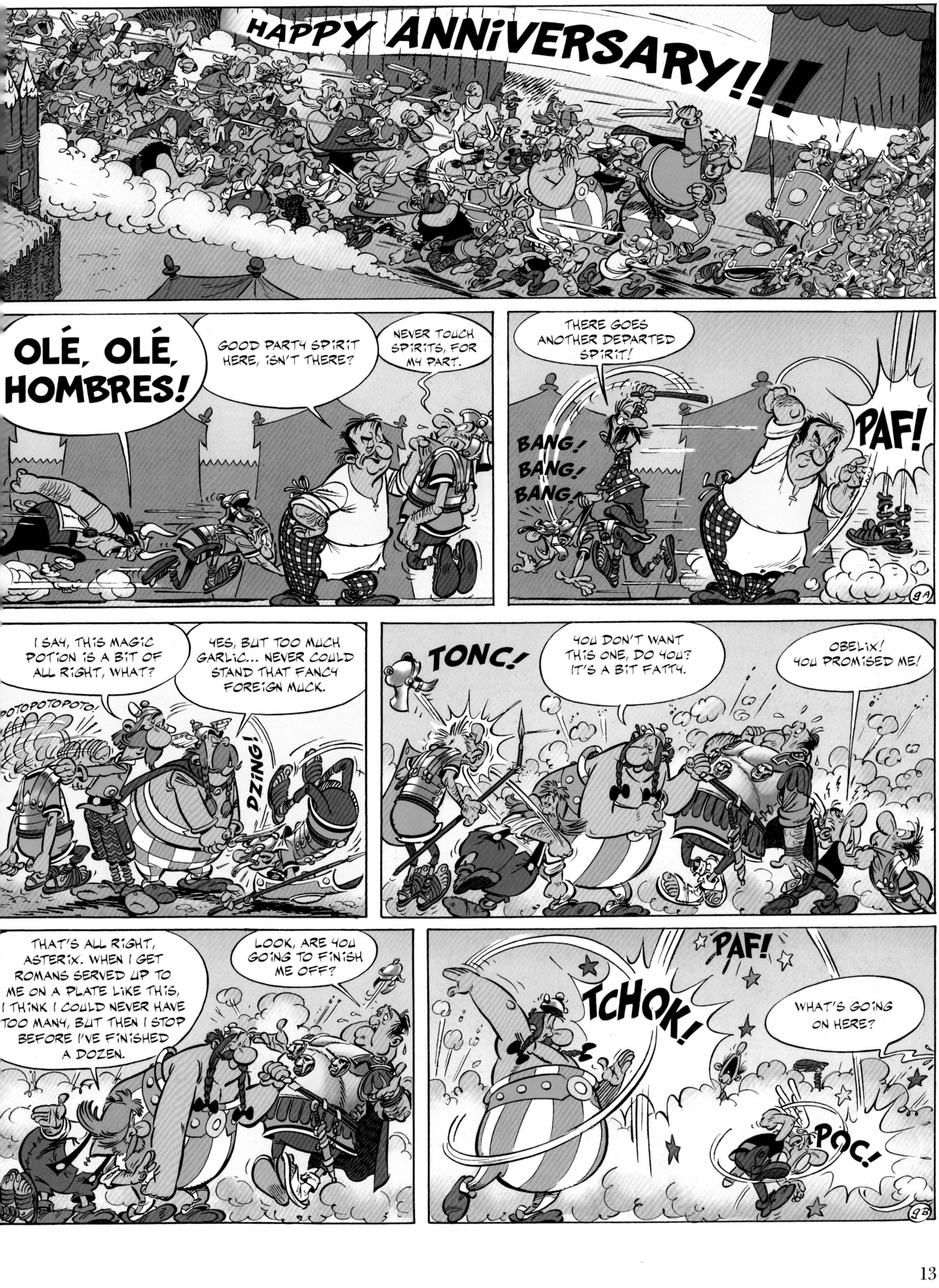
HAPPY ANNiVERSARY!!!
OLÉ, OLÉ, HOMBRES!
GOOD PARTY SPIRIT HERE, ISN'T THERE?
NEVER TOUCH SPIRITS, FOR MY PART.
THERE GOES ANOTHER DEPARTED SPIRIT!
BANG! BANG! BANG!
PAF!
I SAY, THIS MAGIC POTION IS A BIT OF ALL RIGHT, WHAT?
YES, BUT TOO MUCH GARLIC... NEVER COULD STAND THAT FANCY FOREIGN MUCK.
POTOPOTOPOTO!
DZING!
TONC!
YOU DON'T WANT THIS ONE, DO YOU? IT'S A BIT FATTY.
OBELIX! YOU PROMISED ME!
THAT'S ALL RIGHT, ASTERIX. WHEN I GET ROMANS SERVED UP TO ME ON A PLATE LIKE THIS, I THINK I COULD NEVER HAVE TOO MANY, BUT THEN I STOP BEFORE I'VE FINISHED A DOZEN.
LOOK, ARE YOU GOING TO FINISH ME OFF?
PAF!
TCHOK!
WHAT'S GOING ON HERE?
POC!

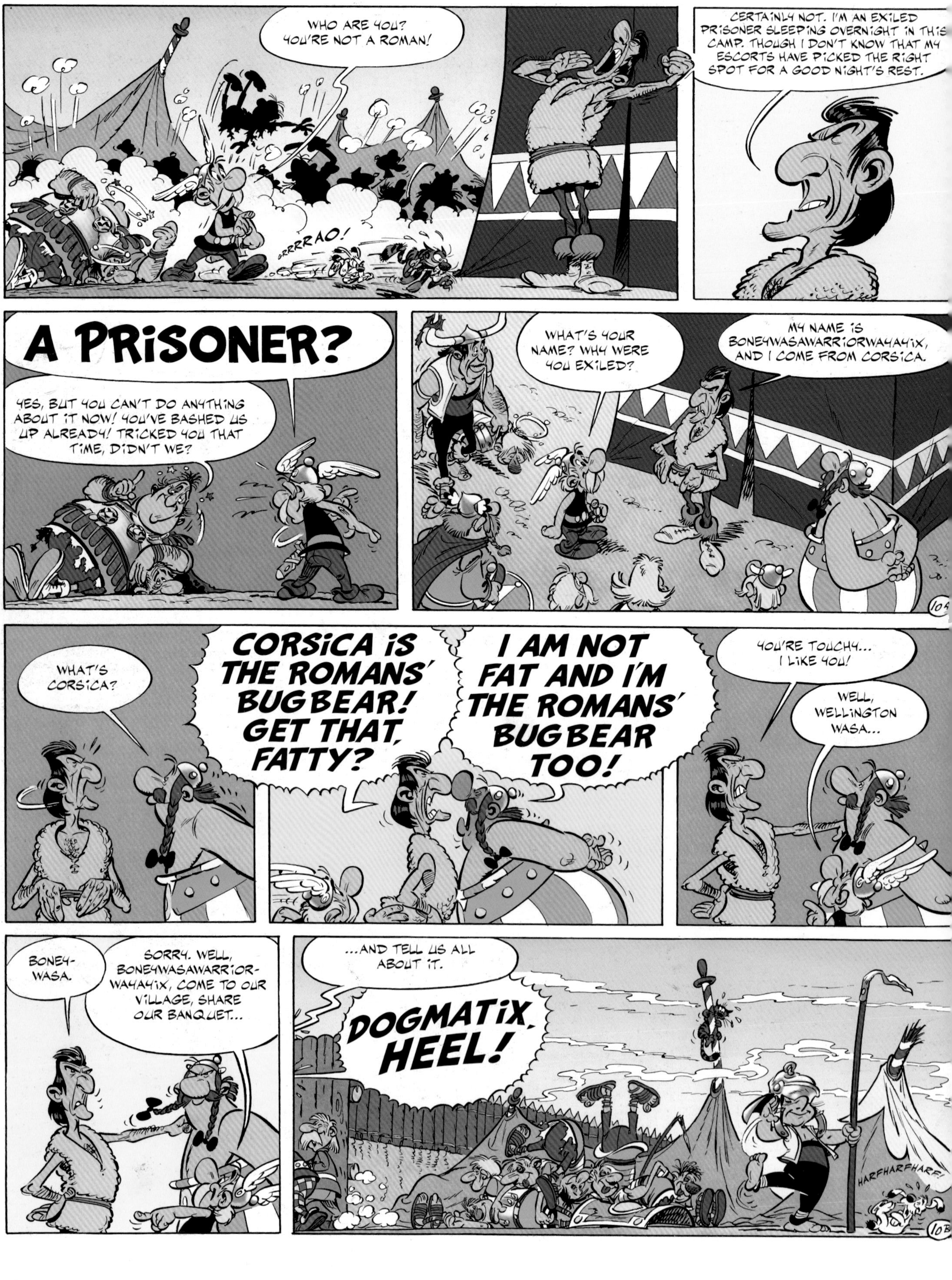

WHO ARE YOU? YOU'RE NOT A ROMAN!
GRRRRAO!
CERTAINLY NOT. I'M AN EXILED PRISONER SLEEPING OVERNIGHT IN THIS CAMP. THOUGH I DON'T KNOW THAT MY ESCORTS HAVE PICKED THE RIGHT SPOT FOR A GOOD NIGHT'S REST.
A PRISONER?
YES, BUT YOU CAN'T DO ANYTHING ABOUT IT NOW! YOU'VE BASHED US UP ALREADY! TRICKED YOU THAT TIME, DIDN'T WE?
WHAT'S YOUR NAME? WHY WERE YOU EXILED?
MY NAME IS BONEYWASAWARRIORWAYAYIX, AND I COME FROM CORSICA.
WHAT'S CORSICA?
CORSICA IS THE ROMANS' BUGBEAR! GET THAT, FATTY?
I AM NOT FAT AND I'M THE ROMANS' BUGBEAR TOO!
YOU'RE TOUCHY... I LIKE YOU!
WELL, WELLINGTON WASA...
BONEY-WASA.
SORRY. WELL, BONEYWASAWARRIOR-WAYAYIX, COME TO OUR VILLAGE, SHARE OUR BANQUET...
...AND TELL US ALL ABOUT IT.
DOGMATIX, HEEL!
HARFHARFHARF!

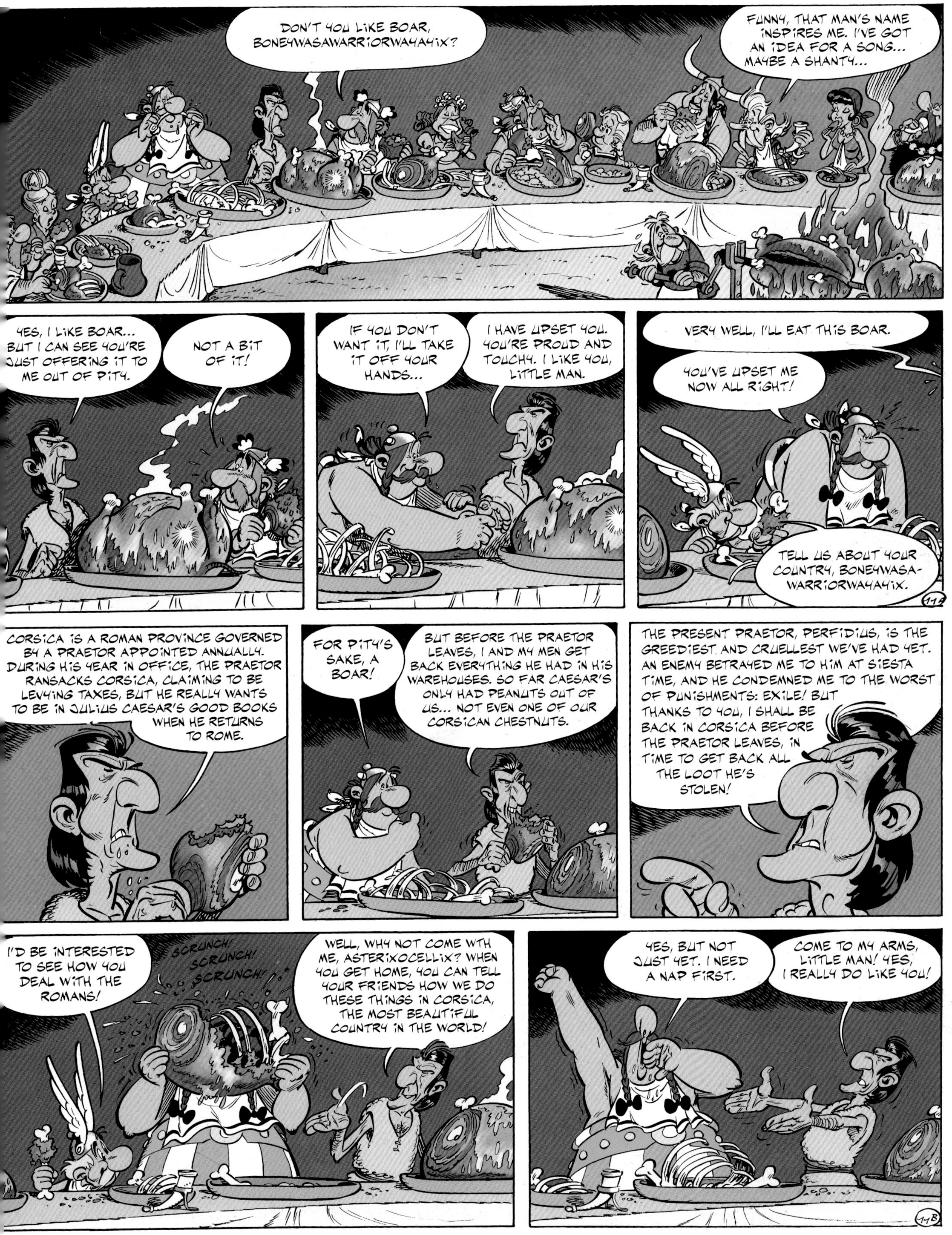
DON'T YOU LIKE BOAR, BONEYWASAWARRIORWAYAYIX?
FUNNY, THAT MAN'S NAME INSPIRES ME. I'VE GOT AN IDEA FOR A SONG... MAYBE A SHANTY...
YES, I LIKE BOAR... BUT I CAN SEE YOU'RE JUST OFFERING IT TO ME OUT OF PITY.
NOT A BIT OF IT!
IF YOU DON'T WANT IT, I'LL TAKE IT OFF YOUR HANDS...
I HAVE UPSET YOU. YOU'RE PROUD AND TOUCHY. I LIKE YOU, LITTLE MAN.
VERY WELL, I'LL EAT THIS BOAR.
YOU'VE UPSET ME NOW ALL RIGHT!
TELL US ABOUT YOUR COUNTRY, BONEYWASA-WARRIORWAYAYIX.
CORSICA IS A ROMAN PROVINCE GOVERNED BY A PRAETOR APPOINTED ANNUALLY. DURING HIS YEAR IN OFFICE, THE PRAETOR RANSACKS CORSICA, CLAIMING TO BE LEVYING TAXES, BUT HE REALLY WANTS TO BE IN JULIUS CAESAR'S GOOD BOOKS WHEN HE RETURNS TO ROME.
FOR PITY'S SAKE, A BOAR!
BUT BEFORE THE PRAETOR LEAVES, I AND MY MEN GET BACK EVERYTHING HE HAD IN HIS WAREHOUSES. SO FAR CAESAR'S ONLY HAD PEANUTS OUT OF US... NOT EVEN ONE OF OUR CORSICAN CHESTNUTS.
THE PRESENT PRAETOR, PERFIDIUS, IS THE GREEDIEST AND CRUELLEST WE'VE HAD YET. AN ENEMY BETRAYED ME TO HIM AT SIESTA TIME, AND HE CONDEMNED ME TO THE WORST OF PUNISHMENTS: EXILE! BUT THANKS TO YOU, I SHALL BE BACK IN CORSICA BEFORE THE PRAETOR LEAVES, IN TIME TO GET BACK ALL THE LOOT HE'S STOLEN!
I'D BE INTERESTED TO SEE HOW YOU DEAL WITH THE ROMANS!
SCRUNCH! SCRUNCH! SCRUNCH!
WELL, WHY NOT COME WITH ME, ASTERIXOCELLIX? WHEN YOU GET HOME, YOU CAN TELL YOUR FRIENDS HOW WE DO THESE THINGS IN CORSICA, THE MOST BEAUTIFUL COUNTRY IN THE WORLD!
YES, BUT NOT JUST YET. I NEED A NAP FIRST.
COME TO MY ARMS, LITTLE MAN! YES, I REALLY DO LIKE YOU!

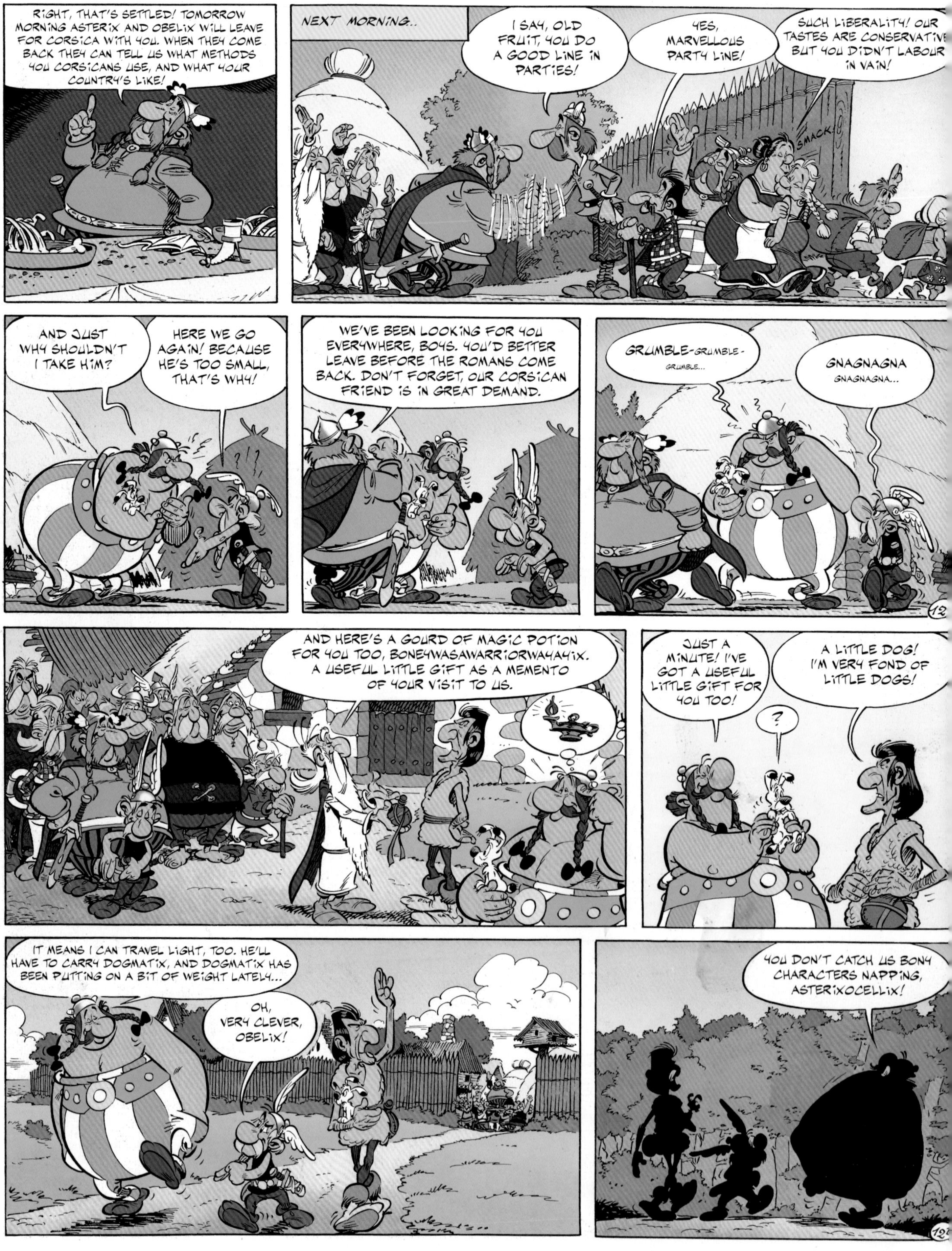
RIGHT, THAT'S SETTLED! TOMORROW MORNING ASTERIX AND OBELIX WILL LEAVE FOR CORSICA WITH YOU. WHEN THEY COME BACK THEY CAN TELL US WHAT METHODS YOU CORSICANS USE, AND WHAT YOUR COUNTRY'S LIKE!
NEXT MORNING...
I SAY, OLD FRUIT, YOU DO A GOOD LINE IN PARTIES!
YES, MARVELLOUS PARTY LINE!
SUCH LIBERALITY! OUR TASTES ARE CONSERVATIVE BUT YOU DIDN'T LABOUR IN VAIN!
SMACK
AND JUST WHY SHOULDN'T I TAKE HIM?
HERE WE GO AGAIN! BECAUSE HE'S TOO SMALL, THAT'S WHY!
WE'VE BEEN LOOKING FOR YOU EVERYWHERE, BOYS. YOU'D BETTER LEAVE BEFORE THE ROMANS COME BACK. DON'T FORGET, OUR CORSICAN FRIEND IS IN GREAT DEMAND.
GRUMBLE-GRUMBLE-GRUMBLE...
GNAGNAGNA GNAGNAGNA...
AND HERE'S A GOURD OF MAGIC POTION FOR YOU TOO, BONEYWASAWARRIORWAYAYIX. A USEFUL LITTLE GIFT AS A MEMENTO OF YOUR VISIT TO US.
JUST A MINUTE! I'VE GOT A USEFUL LITTLE GIFT FOR YOU TOO!
?
A LITTLE DOG! I'M VERY FOND OF LITTLE DOGS!
IT MEANS I CAN TRAVEL LIGHT, TOO. HE'LL HAVE TO CARRY DOGMATIX, AND DOGMATIX HAS BEEN PUTTING ON A BIT OF WEIGHT LATELY...
OH, VERY CLEVER, OBELIX!
YOU DON'T CATCH US BONY CHARACTERS NAPPING, ASTERIXOCELLIX!

THE PORT OF MASSILIA...

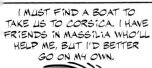

I MUST FIND A BOAT TO TAKE US TO CORSICA. I HAVE FRIENDS IN MASSILIA WHO'LL HELP ME, BUT I'D BETTER GO ON MY OWN.

WE'LL MEET HERE IN AN HOUR'S TIME. HOLD THIS DOG FOR ME, I'M RATHER TIRED.

VERMICELLIX

BONEYWASA-WARRIORWAYAYIX, I AM BESIDE MYSELF WITH JOY.

VERMICELLIX, THE SIGHT OF YOU FILLS ME WITH PLEASURE.

MORTADELLA, LET'S HAVE SOME WINE AND SOME SAUSAGE. NOT THE STUFF WE GIVE THE CUSTOMERS.

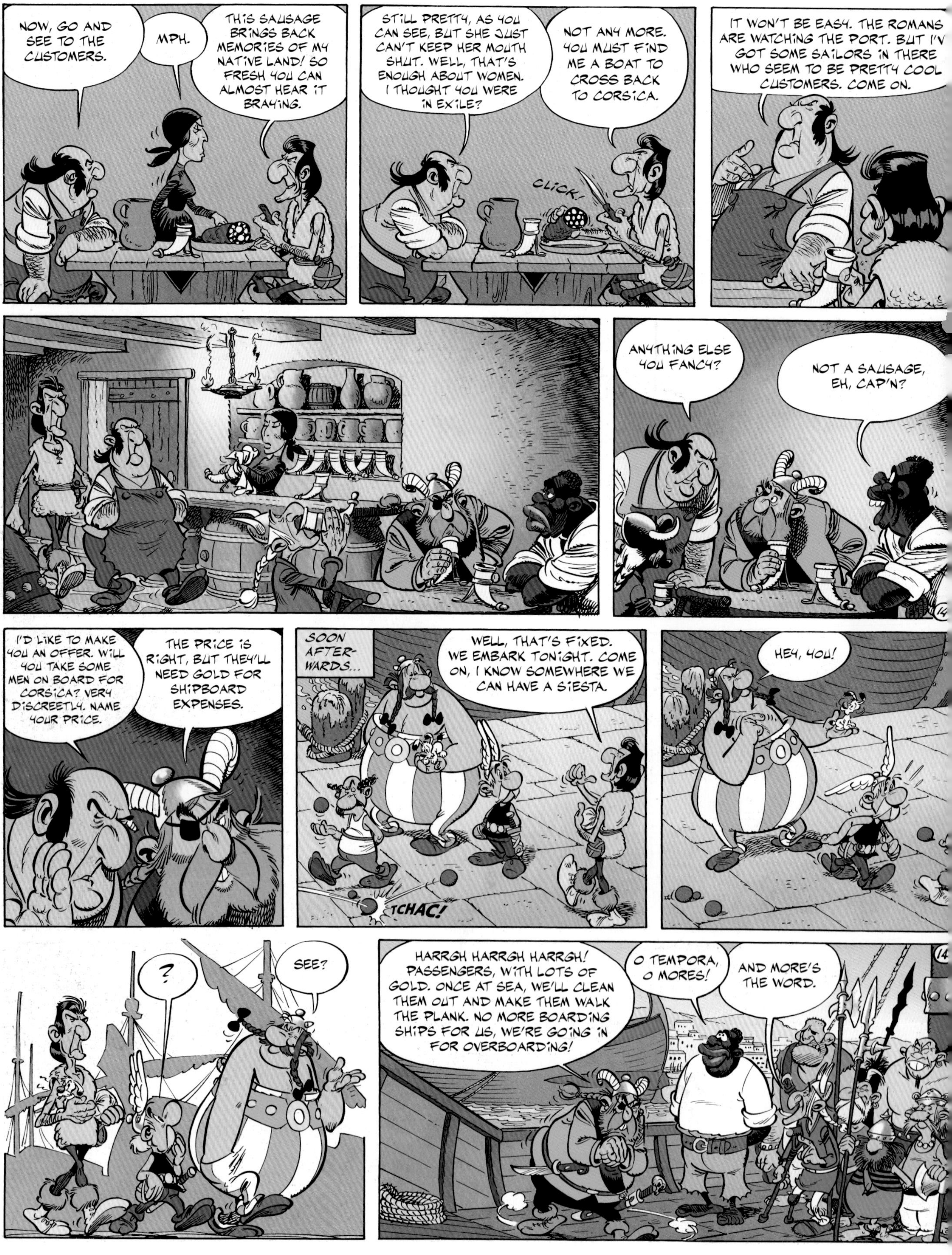
NOW, GO AND SEE TO THE CUSTOMERS.
MPH.
THIS SAUSAGE BRINGS BACK MEMORIES OF MY NATIVE LAND! SO FRESH YOU CAN ALMOST HEAR IT BRAYING.
STILL PRETTY, AS YOU CAN SEE, BUT SHE JUST CAN'T KEEP HER MOUTH SHUT. WELL, THAT'S ENOUGH ABOUT WOMEN. I THOUGHT YOU WERE IN EXILE?
CLICK!
NOT ANY MORE. YOU MUST FIND ME A BOAT TO CROSS BACK TO CORSICA.
IT WON'T BE EASY. THE ROMANS ARE WATCHING THE PORT. BUT I'V GOT SOME SAILORS IN THERE WHO SEEM TO BE PRETTY COOL CUSTOMERS. COME ON.
ANYTHING ELSE YOU FANCY?
NOT A SAUSAGE, EH, CAP'N?
I'D LIKE TO MAKE YOU AN OFFER. WILL YOU TAKE SOME MEN ON BOARD FOR CORSICA? VERY DISCREETLY. NAME YOUR PRICE.
THE PRICE IS RIGHT, BUT THEY'LL NEED GOLD FOR SHIPBOARD EXPENSES.
SOON AFTERWARDS...
WELL, THAT'S FIXED. WE EMBARK TONIGHT. COME ON, I KNOW SOMEWHERE WE CAN HAVE A SIESTA.
TCHAC!
HEY, YOU!
?
SEE?
HARRGH HARRGH HARRGH! PASSENGERS, WITH LOTS OF GOLD. ONCE AT SEA, WE'LL CLEAN THEM OUT AND MAKE THEM WALK THE PLANK. NO MORE BOARDING SHIPS FOR US, WE'RE GOING IN FOR OVERBOARDING!
O TEMPORA, O MORES!
AND MORE'S THE WORD.

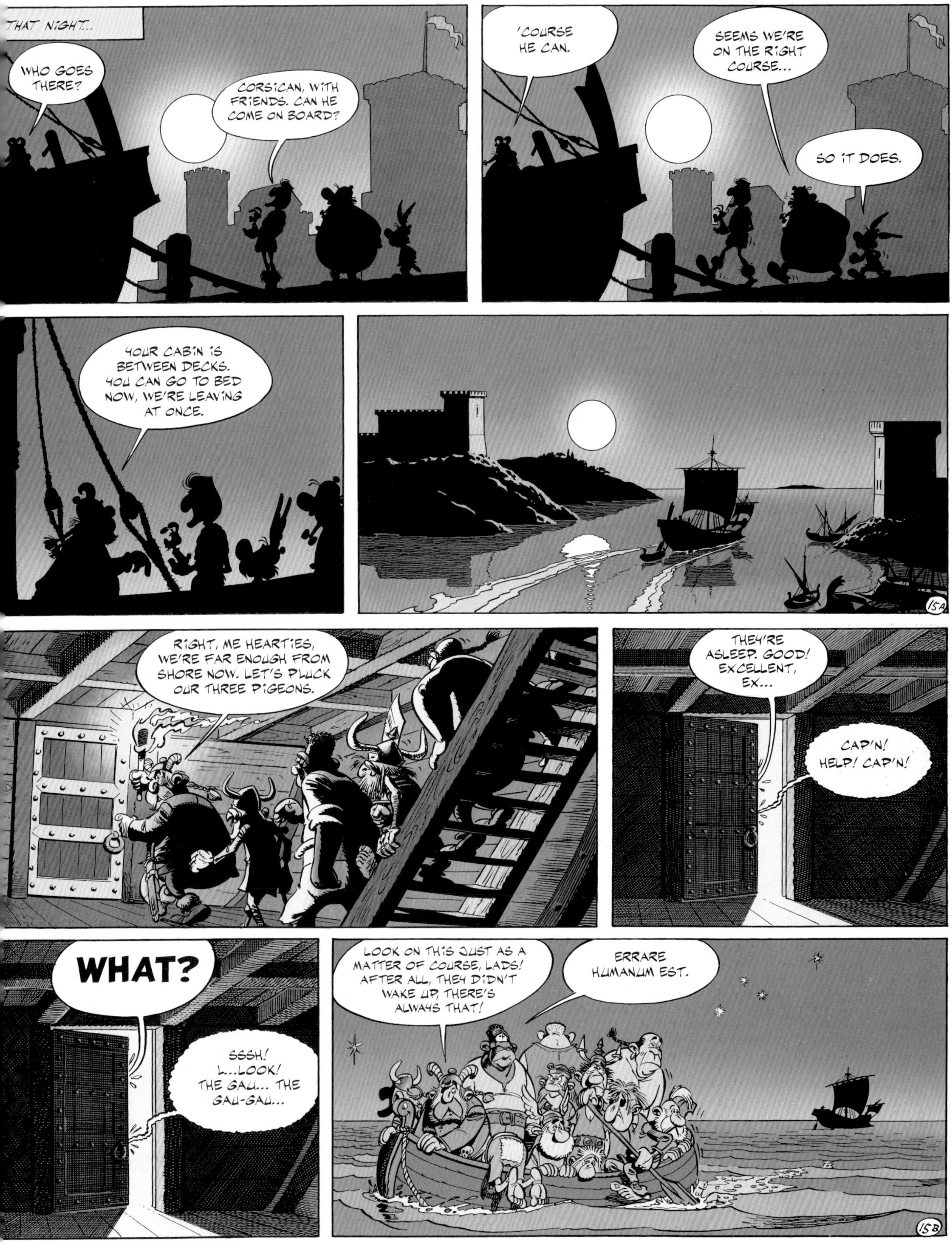
THAT NIGHT...
WHO GOES THERE?
CORSICAN, WITH FRIENDS. CAN HE COME ON BOARD?
'COURSE HE CAN.
SEEMS WE'RE ON THE RIGHT COURSE...
SO IT DOES.
YOUR CABIN IS BETWEEN DECKS. YOU CAN GO TO BED NOW, WE'RE LEAVING AT ONCE.
15A
RIGHT, ME HEARTIES, WE'RE FAR ENOUGH FROM SHORE NOW. LET'S PLUCK OUR THREE PIGEONS.
THEY'RE ASLEEP. GOOD! EXCELLENT, EX...
CAP'N! HELP! CAP'N!
WHAT?
SSSH! L...LOOK! THE GAU... THE GAU-GAU...
LOOK ON THIS JUST AS A MATTER OF COURSE, LADS! AFTER ALL, THEY DIDN'T WAKE UP, THERE'S ALWAYS THAT!
ERRARE HUMANUM EST.
15B

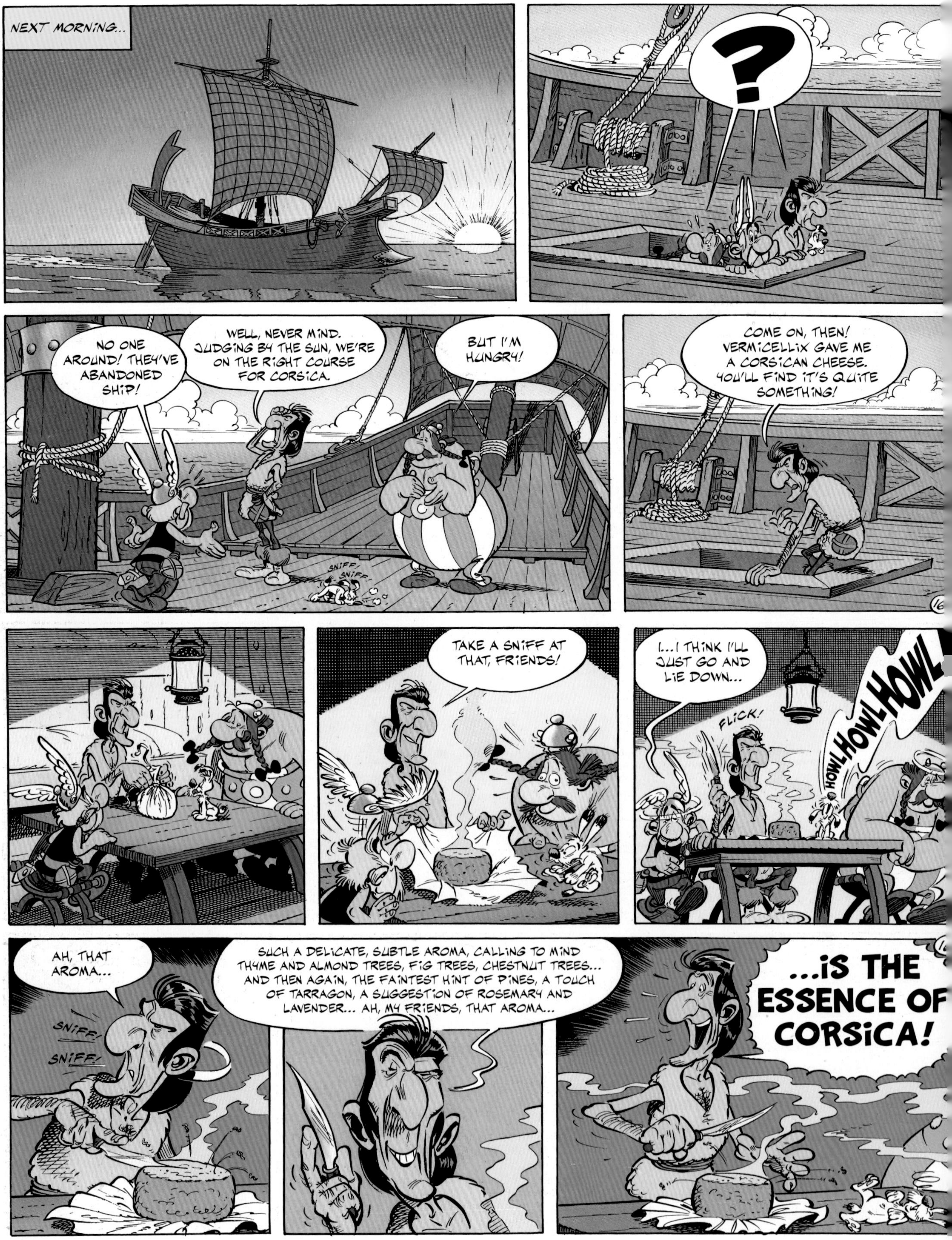

NEXT MORNING...
?
NO ONE AROUND! THEY'VE ABANDONED SHIP!
WELL, NEVER MIND. JUDGING BY THE SUN, WE'RE ON THE RIGHT COURSE FOR CORSICA.
BUT I'M HUNGRY!
SNIFF! SNIFF!
COME ON, THEN! VERMICELLIX GAVE ME A CORSICAN CHEESE. YOU'LL FIND IT'S QUITE SOMETHING!
TAKE A SNIFF AT THAT, FRIENDS!
I...I THINK I'LL JUST GO AND LIE DOWN...
FLICK!
HOWL! HOWL! HOWL!
AH, THAT AROMA...
SNIFF! SNIFF!
SUCH A DELICATE, SUBTLE AROMA, CALLING TO MIND THYME AND ALMOND TREES, FIG TREES, CHESTNUT TREES... AND THEN AGAIN, THE FAINTEST HINT OF PINES, A TOUCH OF TARRAGON, A SUGGESTION OF ROSEMARY AND LAVENDER... AH, MY FRIENDS, THAT AROMA...
...IS THE ESSENCE OF CORSICA!

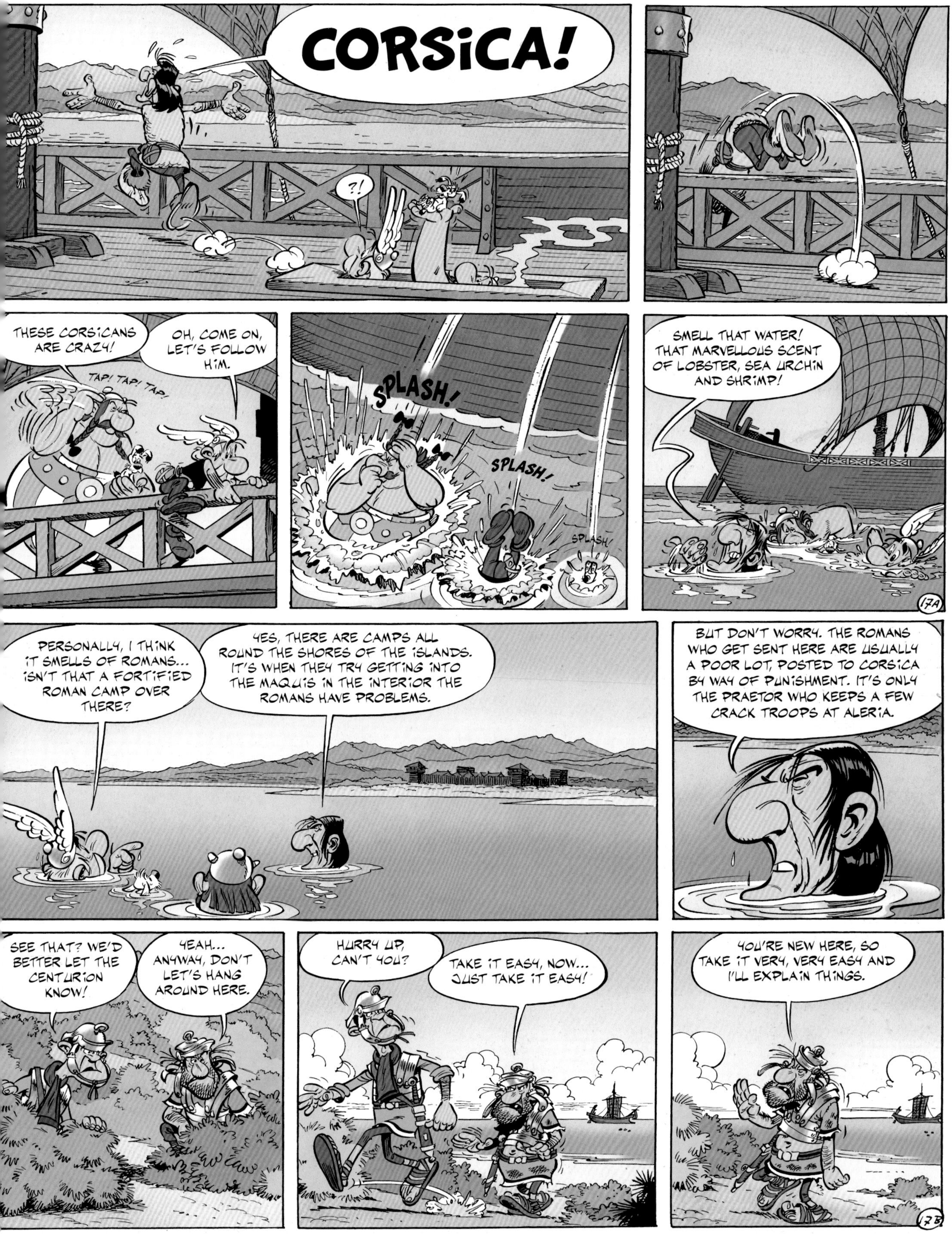
CORSICA!
?!
THESE CORSICANS ARE CRAZY!
TAP! TAP! TAP! TAP!
OH, COME ON, LET'S FOLLOW HIM.
SPLASH!
SPLASH!
SPLASH!
SMELL THAT WATER! THAT MARVELLOUS SCENT OF LOBSTER, SEA URCHIN AND SHRIMP!
17A
PERSONALLY, I THINK IT SMELLS OF ROMANS... ISN'T THAT A FORTIFIED ROMAN CAMP OVER THERE?
YES, THERE ARE CAMPS ALL ROUND THE SHORES OF THE ISLANDS. IT'S WHEN THEY TRY GETTING INTO THE MAQUIS IN THE INTERIOR THE ROMANS HAVE PROBLEMS.
BUT DON'T WORRY. THE ROMANS WHO GET SENT HERE ARE USUALLY A POOR LOT, POSTED TO CORSICA BY WAY OF PUNISHMENT. IT'S ONLY THE PRAETOR WHO KEEPS A FEW CRACK TROOPS AT ALERIA.
SEE THAT? WE'D BETTER LET THE CENTURION KNOW!
YEAH... ANYWAY, DON'T LET'S HANG AROUND HERE.
HURRY UP, CAN'T YOU?
TAKE IT EASY, NOW... JUST TAKE IT EASY!
YOU'RE NEW HERE, SO TAKE IT VERY, VERY EASY AND I'LL EXPLAIN THINGS.
17B

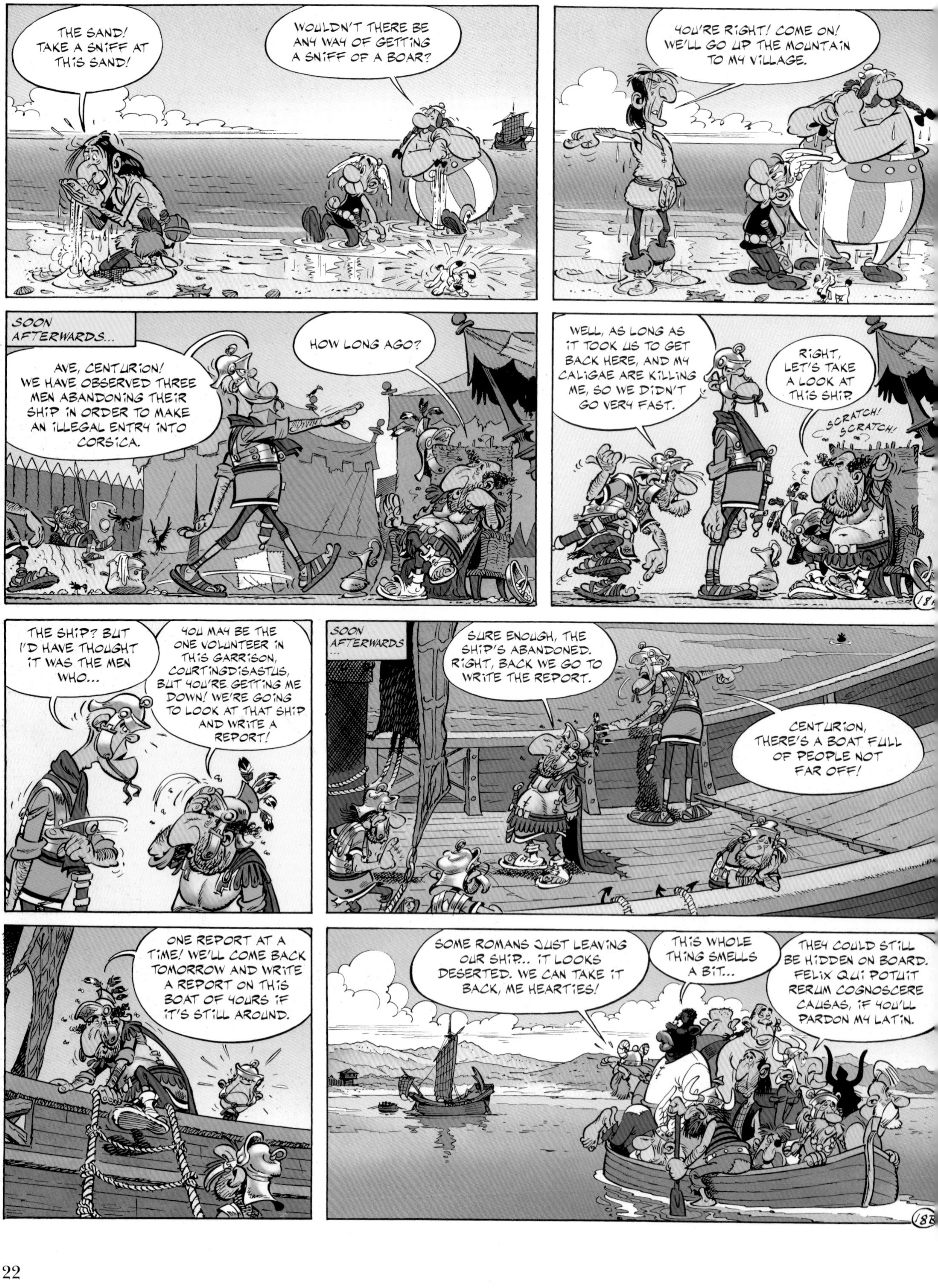
THE SAND! TAKE A SNIFF AT THIS SAND!
WOULDN'T THERE BE ANY WAY OF GETTING A SNIFF OF A BOAR?
YOU'RE RIGHT! COME ON! WE'LL GO UP THE MOUNTAIN TO MY VILLAGE.
SOON AFTERWARDS...
AVE, CENTURION! WE HAVE OBSERVED THREE MEN ABANDONING THEIR SHIP IN ORDER TO MAKE AN ILLEGAL ENTRY INTO CORSICA.
HOW LONG AGO?
WELL, AS LONG AS IT TOOK US TO GET BACK HERE, AND MY CALIGAE ARE KILLING ME, SO WE DIDN'T GO VERY FAST.
RIGHT, LET'S TAKE A LOOK AT THIS SHIP.
SCRATCH! SCRATCH!
THE SHIP? BUT I'D HAVE THOUGHT IT WAS THE MEN WHO...
YOU MAY BE THE ONE VOLUNTEER IN THIS GARRISON, COURTINGDISASTUS, BUT YOU'RE GETTING ME DOWN! WE'RE GOING TO LOOK AT THAT SHIP AND WRITE A REPORT!
SOON AFTERWARDS...
SURE ENOUGH, THE SHIP'S ABANDONED. RIGHT, BACK WE GO TO WRITE THE REPORT.
CENTURION, THERE'S A BOAT FULL OF PEOPLE NOT FAR OFF!
ONE REPORT AT A TIME! WE'LL COME BACK TOMORROW AND WRITE A REPORT ON THIS BOAT OF YOURS IF IT'S STILL AROUND.
SOME ROMANS JUST LEAVING OUR SHIP.. IT LOOKS DESERTED. WE CAN TAKE IT BACK, ME HEARTIES!
THIS WHOLE THING SMELLS A BIT...
THEY COULD STILL BE HIDDEN ON BOARD. FELIX QUI POTUIT RERUM COGNOSCERE CAUSAS, IF YOU'LL PARDON MY LATIN.

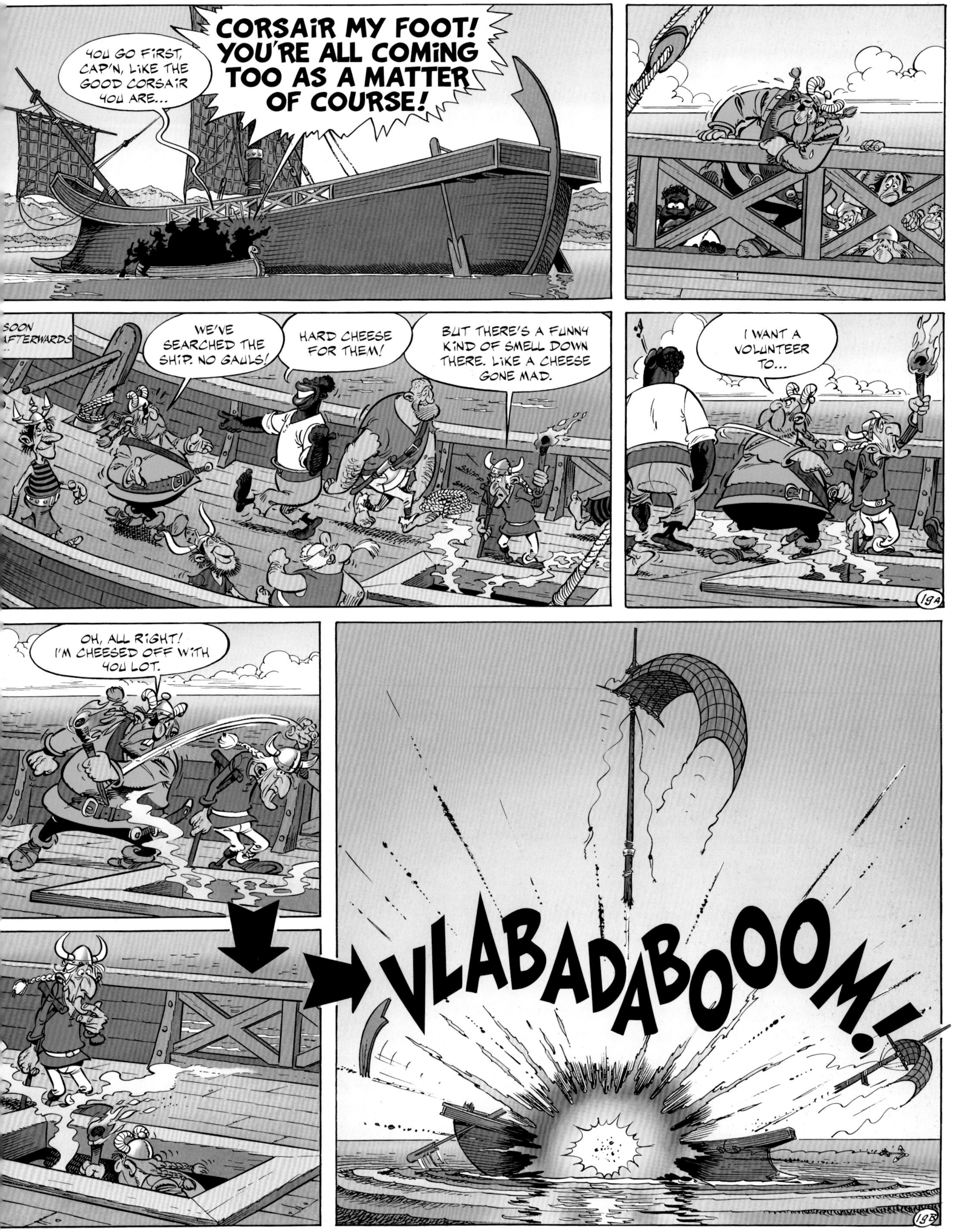

YOU GO FIRST, CAP'N, LIKE THE GOOD CORSAIR YOU ARE...
CORSAIR MY FOOT! YOU'RE ALL COMING TOO AS A MATTER OF COURSE!
SOON AFTERWARDS
WE'VE SEARCHED THE SHIP. NO GAULS!
HARD CHEESE FOR THEM!
BUT THERE'S A FUNNY KIND OF SMELL DOWN THERE. LIKE A CHEESE GONE MAD.
SNIFF
SNIFF
I WANT A VOLUNTEER TO...
OH, ALL RIGHT! I'M CHEESED OFF WITH YOU LOT.
VLABADABOOOM!

RIGHT, THERE'S NOTHING LEFT FOR US TO DO HERE. WE'RE OFF.

WHAT DO YOU MEAN, WE'RE OFF? WHAT ABOUT THIS?

WELL, WHAT ABOUT IT? A SHIP ARRIVES, THREE CHARACTERS DIVE INTO THE SEA, THE SHIP'S ABANDONED, IT BLOWS UP, ANOTHER SET OF CHARACTERS COME SWIMMING ASHORE...

MERE COMMONPLACE. HARDLY WORTH WRITING A REPORT AT ALL.

I DISAGREE, CENTURION. WE OUGHT TO WARN PRAETOR PERFIDIUS AT ALERIA!

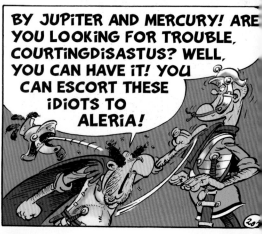

BY JUPITER AND MERCURY! ARE YOU LOOKING FOR TROUBLE, COURTINGDISASTUS? WELL, YOU CAN HAVE IT! YOU CAN ESCORT THESE IDIOTS TO ALERIA!

MEANWHILE...

MY VILLAGE IS QUITE CLOSE.

IS HE FROM YOUR VILLAGE?

YES, THAT'S LETHARGIX OUR DRUID. HE'S BUSY GATHERING MISTLETOE.

THAT'S THE WAY HE GATHERS MISTLETOE?

YES, HE'S WAITING FOR IT TO FALL OFF THE TREE.

TOC! TOC! TOC! TOC!

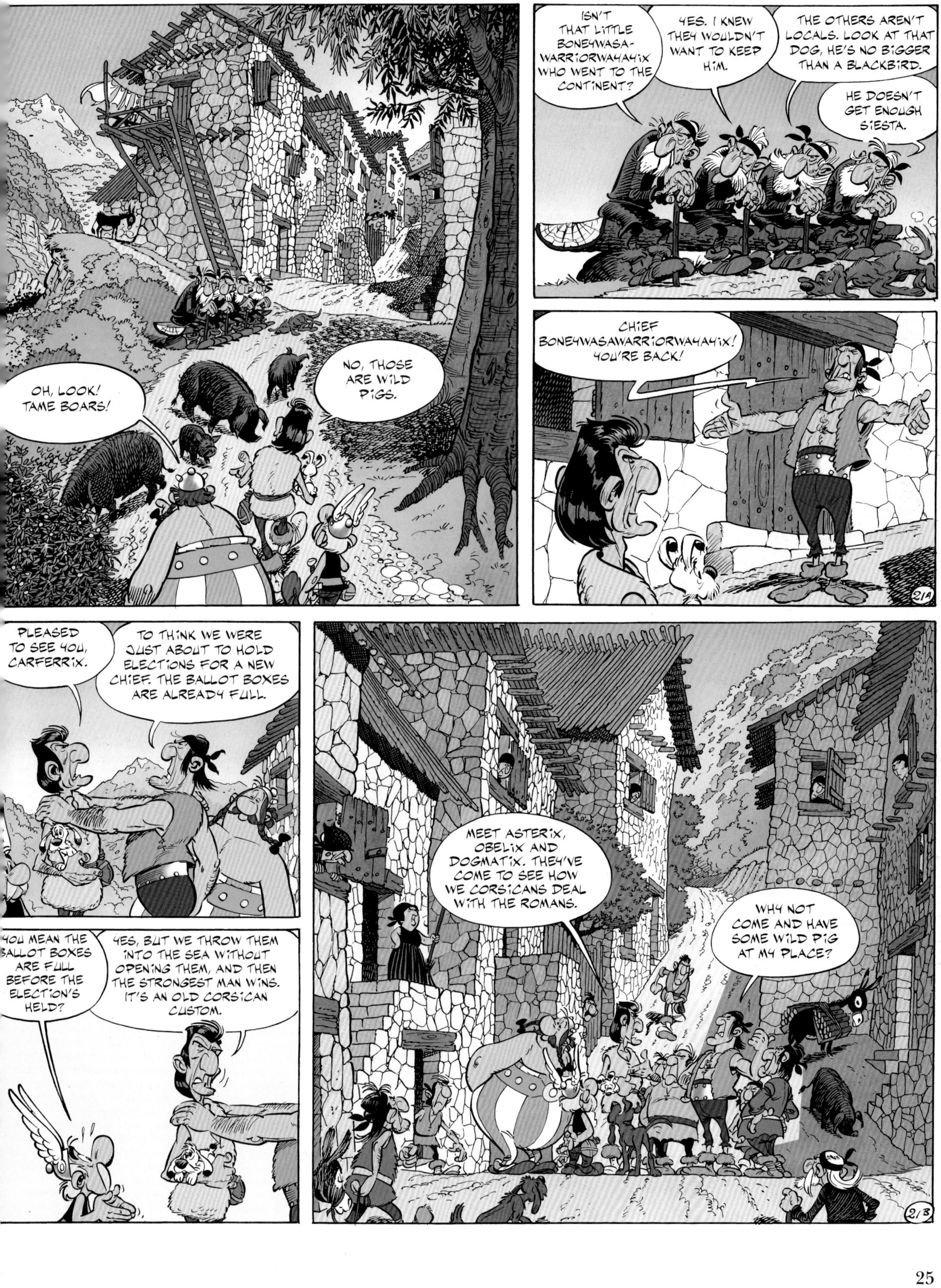

OH, LOOK! TAME BOARS!
NO, THOSE ARE WILD PIGS.
ISN'T THAT LITTLE BONEYWASA-WARRIORWAYAYIX WHO WENT TO THE CONTINENT?
YES. I KNEW THEY WOULDN'T WANT TO KEEP HIM.
THE OTHERS AREN'T LOCALS. LOOK AT THAT DOG, HE'S NO BIGGER THAN A BLACKBIRD.
HE DOESN'T GET ENOUGH SIESTA.
CHIEF BONEYWASAWARRIORWAYAYIX! YOU'RE BACK!
21A
PLEASED TO SEE YOU, CARFERRIX.
TO THINK WE WERE JUST ABOUT TO HOLD ELECTIONS FOR A NEW CHIEF. THE BALLOT BOXES ARE ALREADY FULL.
YOU MEAN THE BALLOT BOXES ARE FULL BEFORE THE ELECTION'S HELD?
YES, BUT WE THROW THEM INTO THE SEA WITHOUT OPENING THEM, AND THEN THE STRONGEST MAN WINS. IT'S AN OLD CORSICAN CUSTOM.
MEET ASTERIX, OBELIX AND DOGMATIX. THEY'VE COME TO SEE HOW WE CORSICANS DEAL WITH THE ROMANS.
WHY NOT COME AND HAVE SOME WILD PIG AT MY PLACE?
21B

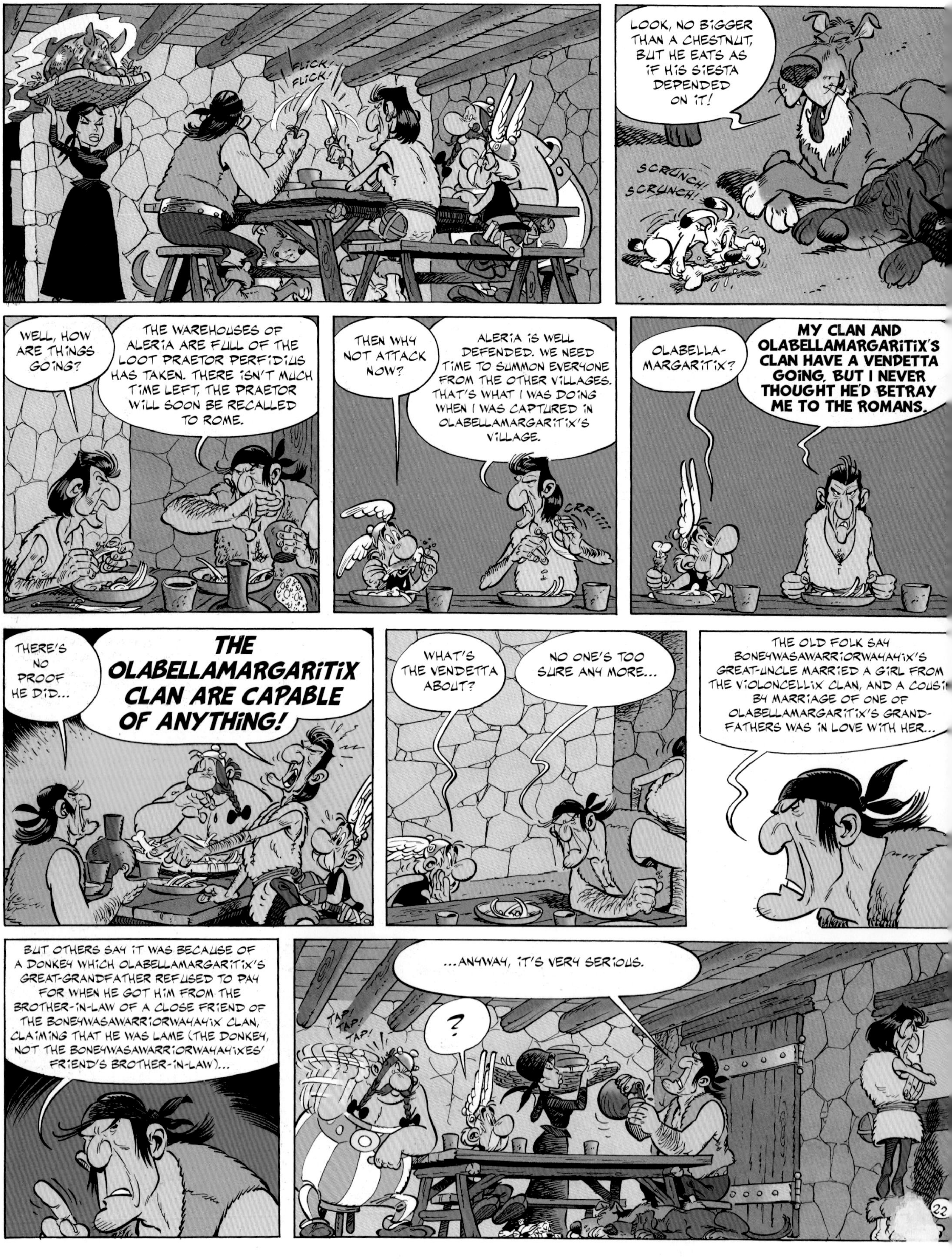

FLICK! FLICK!
LOOK, NO BIGGER THAN A CHESTNUT, BUT HE EATS AS IF HIS SIESTA DEPENDED ON IT!
SCRUNCH! SCRUNCH!
WELL, HOW ARE THINGS GOING?
THE WAREHOUSES OF ALERIA ARE FULL OF THE LOOT PRAETOR PERFIDIUS HAS TAKEN. THERE ISN'T MUCH TIME LEFT, THE PRAETOR WILL SOON BE RECALLED TO ROME.
THEN WHY NOT ATTACK NOW?
ALERIA IS WELL DEFENDED. WE NEED TIME TO SUMMON EVERYONE FROM THE OTHER VILLAGES. THAT'S WHAT I WAS DOING WHEN I WAS CAPTURED IN OLABELLAMARGARITIX'S VILLAGE.
CRR!!!!
OLABELLA-MARGARITIX?
MY CLAN AND OLABELLAMARGARITIX'S CLAN HAVE A VENDETTA GOING, BUT I NEVER THOUGHT HE'D BETRAY ME TO THE ROMANS.
THERE'S NO PROOF HE DID...
THE OLABELLAMARGARITIX CLAN ARE CAPABLE OF ANYTHING!
WHAT'S THE VENDETTA ABOUT?
NO ONE'S TOO SURE ANY MORE...
THE OLD FOLK SAY BONEYWASAWARRIORWAYAYIX'S GREAT-UNCLE MARRIED A GIRL FROM THE VIOLONCELLIX CLAN, AND A COUSIN BY MARRIAGE OF ONE OF OLABELLAMARGARITIX'S GRAND-FATHERS WAS IN LOVE WITH HER...
BUT OTHERS SAY IT WAS BECAUSE OF A DONKEY WHICH OLABELLAMARGARITIX'S GREAT-GRANDFATHER REFUSED TO PAY FOR WHEN HE GOT HIM FROM THE BROTHER-IN-LAW OF A CLOSE FRIEND OF THE BONEYWASAWARRIORWAYAYIX CLAN, CLAIMING THAT HE WAS LAME (THE DONKEY, NOT THE BONEYWASAWARRIORWAYAYIXES' FRIEND'S BROTHER-IN-LAW)...
...ANYWAY, IT'S VERY SERIOUS.
TAP! TAP! TAP!
?
22

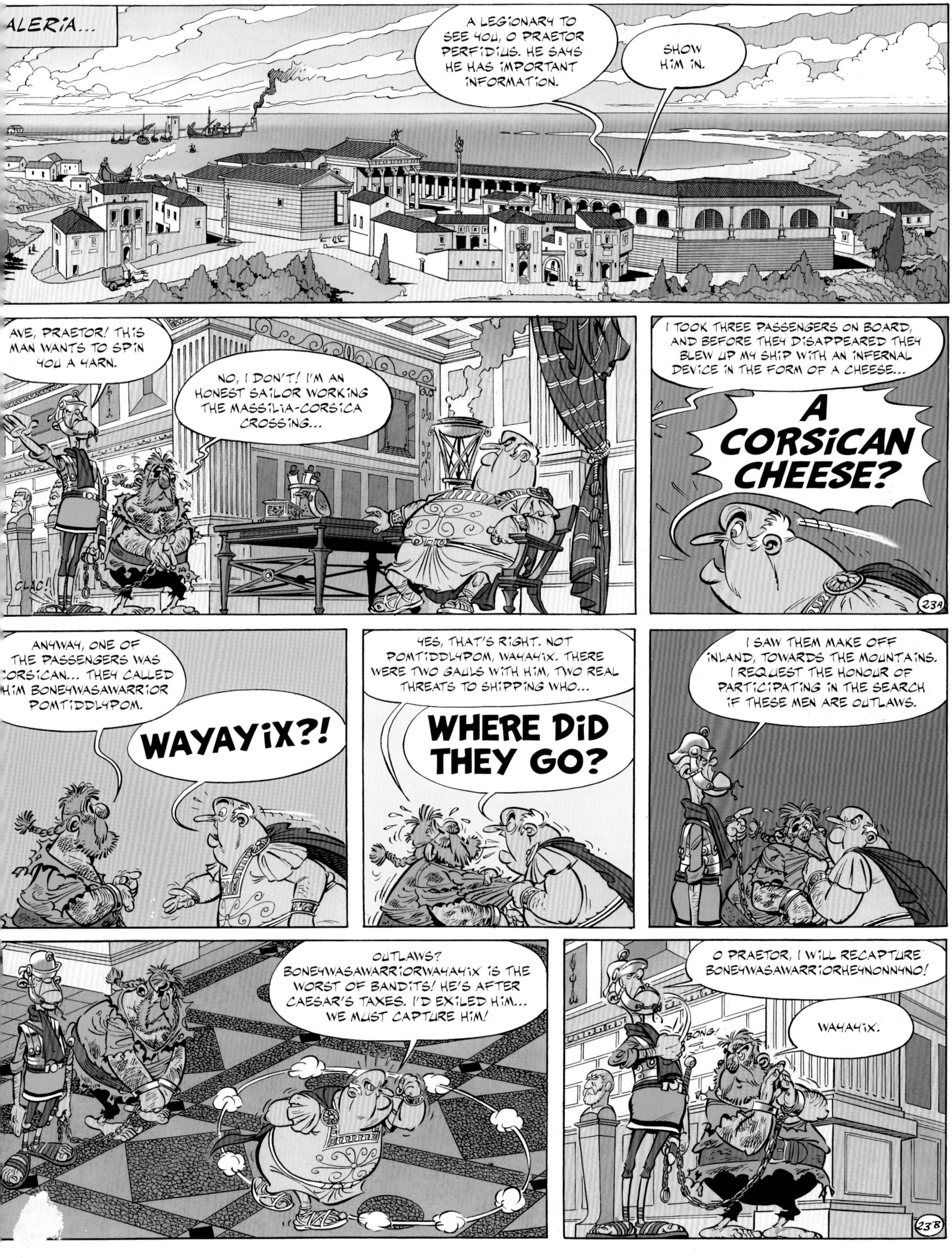
ALERIA...
A LEGIONARY TO SEE YOU, O PRAETOR PERFIDIUS. HE SAYS HE HAS IMPORTANT INFORMATION.
SHOW HIM IN.
AVE, PRAETOR! THIS MAN WANTS TO SPIN YOU A YARN.
NO, I DON'T! I'M AN HONEST SAILOR WORKING THE MASSILIA-CORSICA CROSSING...
CLAC!
I TOOK THREE PASSENGERS ON BOARD, AND BEFORE THEY DISAPPEARED THEY BLEW UP MY SHIP WITH AN INFERNAL DEVICE IN THE FORM OF A CHEESE...
A CORSICAN CHEESE?
23A
ANYWAY, ONE OF THE PASSENGERS WAS CORSICAN... THEY CALLED HIM BONEYWASAWARRIOR POMTIDDLYPOM.
WAYAYIX?!
YES, THAT'S RIGHT. NOT POMTIDDLYPOM, WAYAYIX. THERE WERE TWO GAULS WITH HIM, TWO REAL THREATS TO SHIPPING WHO...
WHERE DID THEY GO?
I SAW THEM MAKE OFF INLAND, TOWARDS THE MOUNTAINS. I REQUEST THE HONOUR OF PARTICIPATING IN THE SEARCH IF THESE MEN ARE OUTLAWS.
OUTLAWS? BONEYWASAWARRIORWAYAYIX IS THE WORST OF BANDITS! HE'S AFTER CAESAR'S TAXES. I'D EXILED HIM... WE MUST CAPTURE HIM!
O PRAETOR, I WILL RECAPTURE BONEYWASAWARRIORHEYNONNYNO!
BONG!
WAYAYIX.
23B

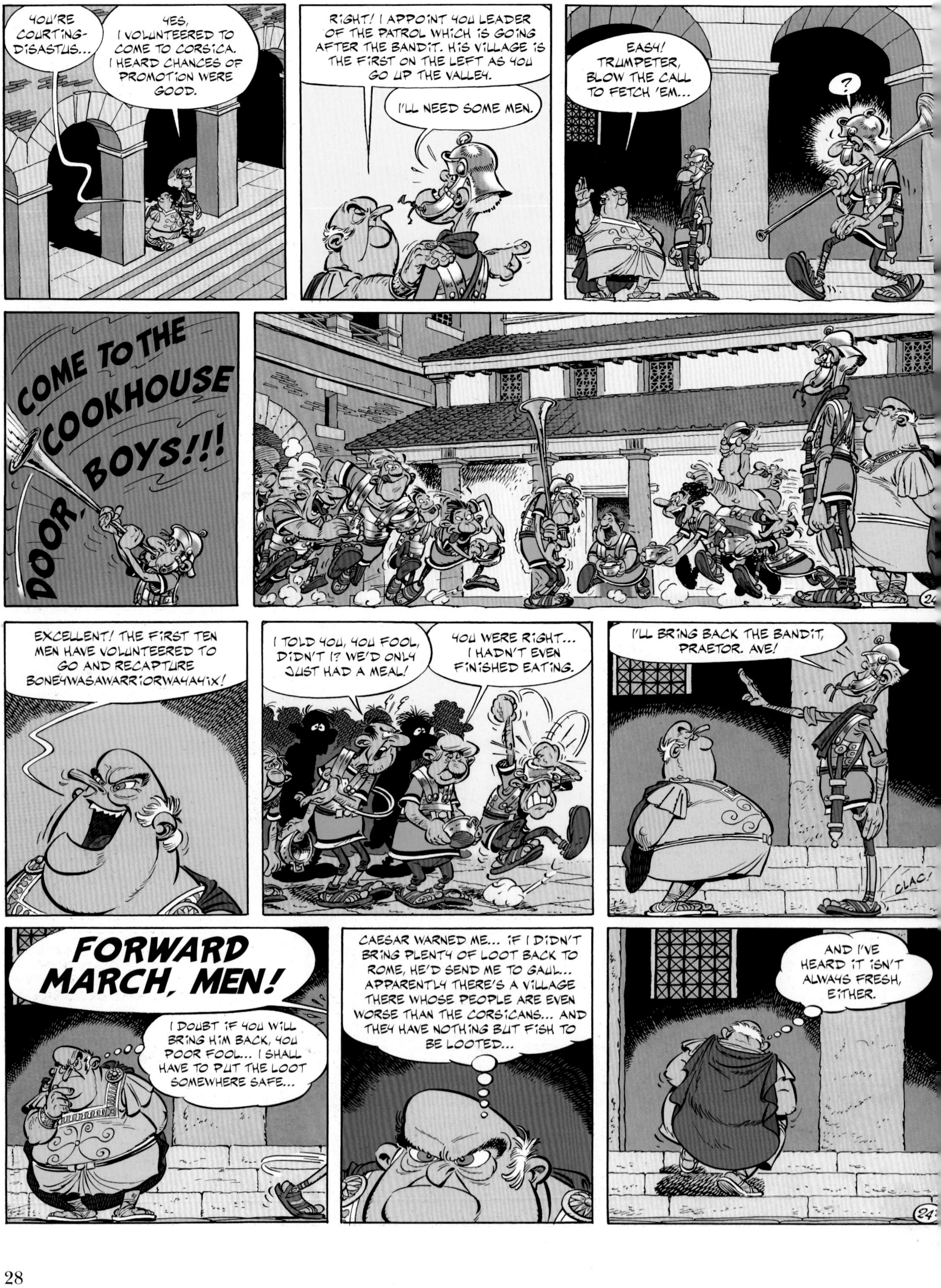

YOU'RE COURTING-DISASTUS...
YES, I VOLUNTEERED TO COME TO CORSICA. I HEARD CHANCES OF PROMOTION WERE GOOD.
RIGHT! I APPOINT YOU LEADER OF THE PATROL WHICH IS GOING AFTER THE BANDIT. HIS VILLAGE IS THE FIRST ON THE LEFT AS YOU GO UP THE VALLEY.
I'LL NEED SOME MEN.
EASY! TRUMPETER, BLOW THE CALL TO FETCH 'EM...
?
COME TO THE COOKHOUSE DOOR, BOYS!!!
EXCELLENT! THE FIRST TEN MEN HAVE VOLUNTEERED TO GO AND RECAPTURE BONEYWASAWARRIORWAYAYIX!
I TOLD YOU, YOU FOOL, DIDN'T I? WE'D ONLY JUST HAD A MEAL!
YOU WERE RIGHT... I HADN'T EVEN FINISHED EATING.
I'LL BRING BACK THE BANDIT, PRAETOR. AVE!
CLAC!
FORWARD MARCH, MEN!
I DOUBT IF YOU WILL BRING HIM BACK, YOU POOR FOOL... I SHALL HAVE TO PUT THE LOOT SOMEWHERE SAFE...
CAESAR WARNED ME... IF I DIDN'T BRING PLENTY OF LOOT BACK TO ROME, HE'D SEND ME TO GAUL... APPARENTLY THERE'S A VILLAGE THERE WHOSE PEOPLE ARE EVEN WORSE THAN THE CORSICANS... AND THEY HAVE NOTHING BUT FISH TO BE LOOTED...
AND I'VE HEARD IT ISN'T ALWAYS FRESH, EITHER.

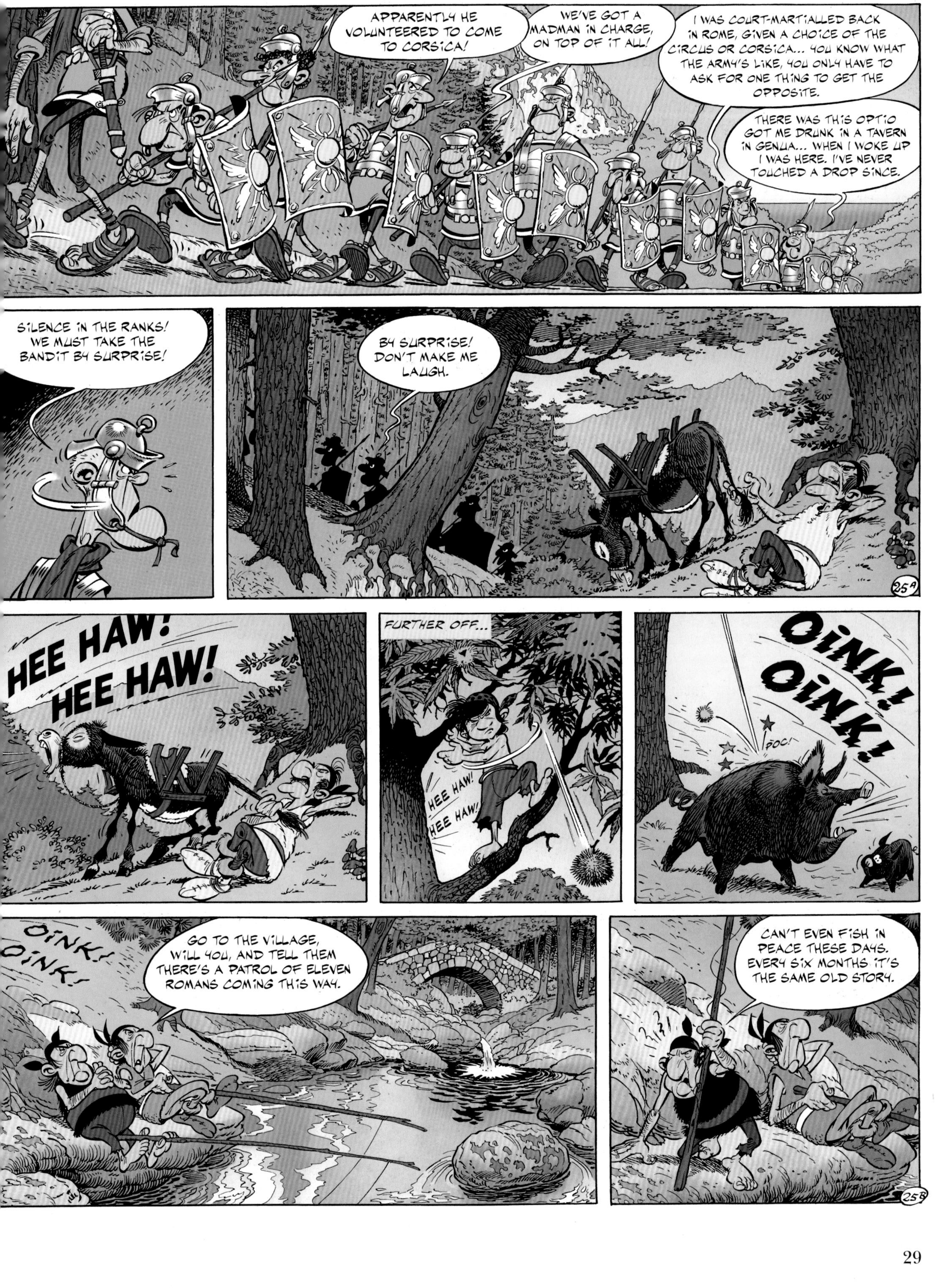
APPARENTLY HE VOLUNTEERED TO COME TO CORSICA!
WE'VE GOT A MADMAN IN CHARGE, ON TOP OF IT ALL!
I WAS COURT-MARTIALLED BACK IN ROME, GIVEN A CHOICE OF THE CIRCUS OR CORSICA... YOU KNOW WHAT THE ARMY'S LIKE, YOU ONLY HAVE TO ASK FOR ONE THING TO GET THE OPPOSITE.
THERE WAS THIS OPTIO GOT ME DRUNK IN A TAVERN IN GENUA... WHEN I WOKE UP I WAS HERE. I'VE NEVER TOUCHED A DROP SINCE.
SILENCE IN THE RANKS! WE MUST TAKE THE BANDIT BY SURPRISE!
BY SURPRISE! DON'T MAKE ME LAUGH.
25A
HEE HAW! HEE HAW!
FURTHER OFF...
HEE HAW! HEE HAW!
OINK! OINK!
POC!
OINK! OINK!
GO TO THE VILLAGE, WILL YOU, AND TELL THEM THERE'S A PATROL OF ELEVEN ROMANS COMING THIS WAY.
CAN'T EVEN FISH IN PEACE THESE DAYS. EVERY SIX MONTHS IT'S THE SAME OLD STORY.
25B

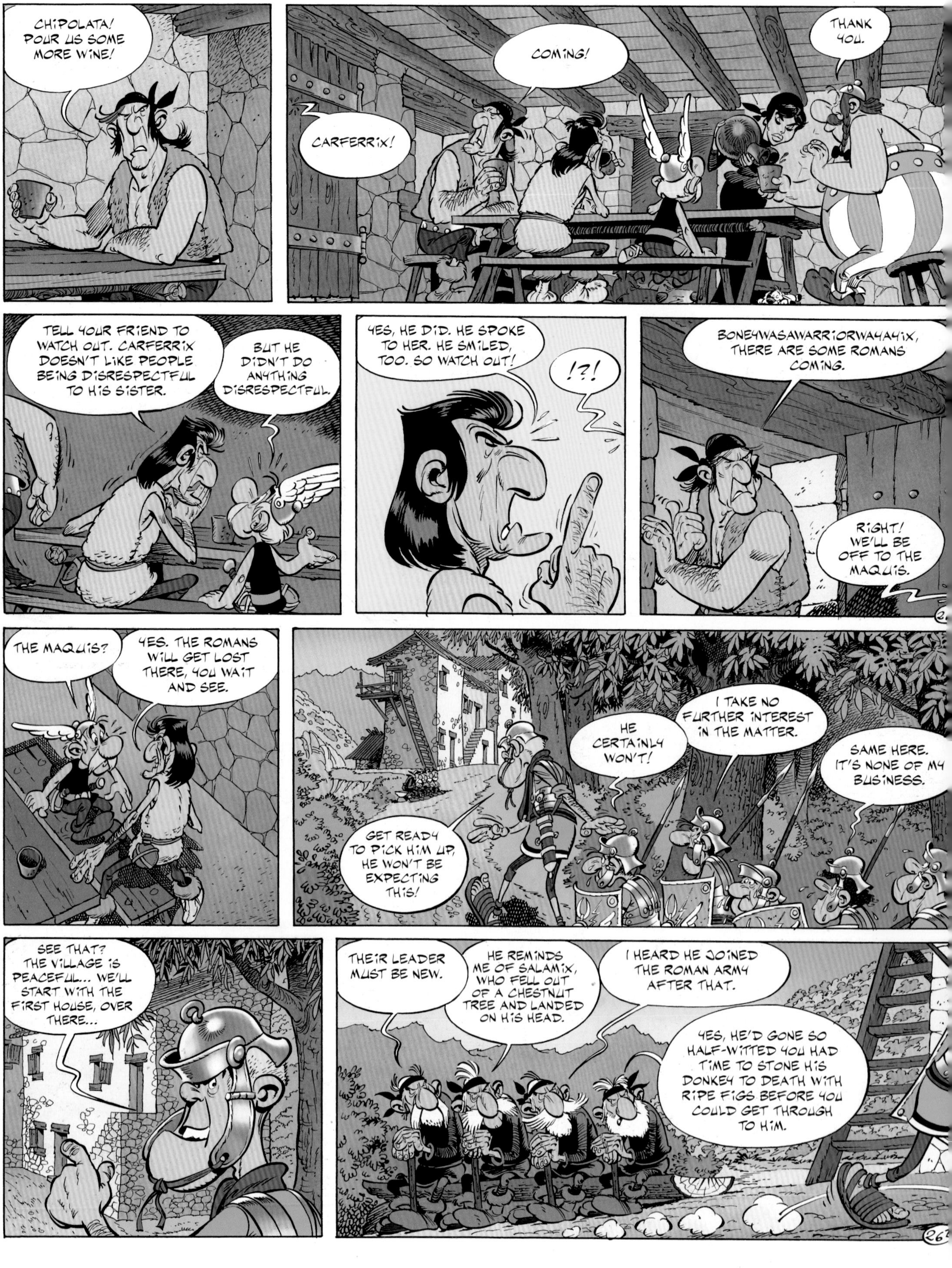
CHIPOLATA! POUR US SOME MORE WINE!
CARFERRIX!
COMING!
THANK YOU.
TELL YOUR FRIEND TO WATCH OUT. CARFERRIX DOESN'T LIKE PEOPLE BEING DISRESPECTFUL TO HIS SISTER.
BUT HE DIDN'T DO ANYTHING DISRESPECTFUL.
YES, HE DID. HE SPOKE TO HER. HE SMILED, TOO. SO WATCH OUT!
!?!
BONEYWASAWARRIORWAYAYIX, THERE ARE SOME ROMANS COMING.
RIGHT! WE'LL BE OFF TO THE MAQUIS.
THE MAQUIS?
YES. THE ROMANS WILL GET LOST THERE, YOU WAIT AND SEE.
GET READY TO PICK HIM UP, HE WON'T BE EXPECTING THIS!
HE CERTAINLY WON'T!
I TAKE NO FURTHER INTEREST IN THE MATTER.
SAME HERE. IT'S NONE OF MY BUSINESS.
SEE THAT? THE VILLAGE IS PEACEFUL... WE'LL START WITH THE FIRST HOUSE, OVER THERE...
THEIR LEADER MUST BE NEW.
HE REMINDS ME OF SALAMIX, WHO FELL OUT OF A CHESTNUT TREE AND LANDED ON HIS HEAD.
I HEARD HE JOINED THE ROMAN ARMY AFTER THAT.
YES, HE'D GONE SO HALF-WITTED YOU HAD TIME TO STONE HIS DONKEY TO DEATH WITH RIPE FIGS BEFORE YOU COULD GET THROUGH TO HIM.

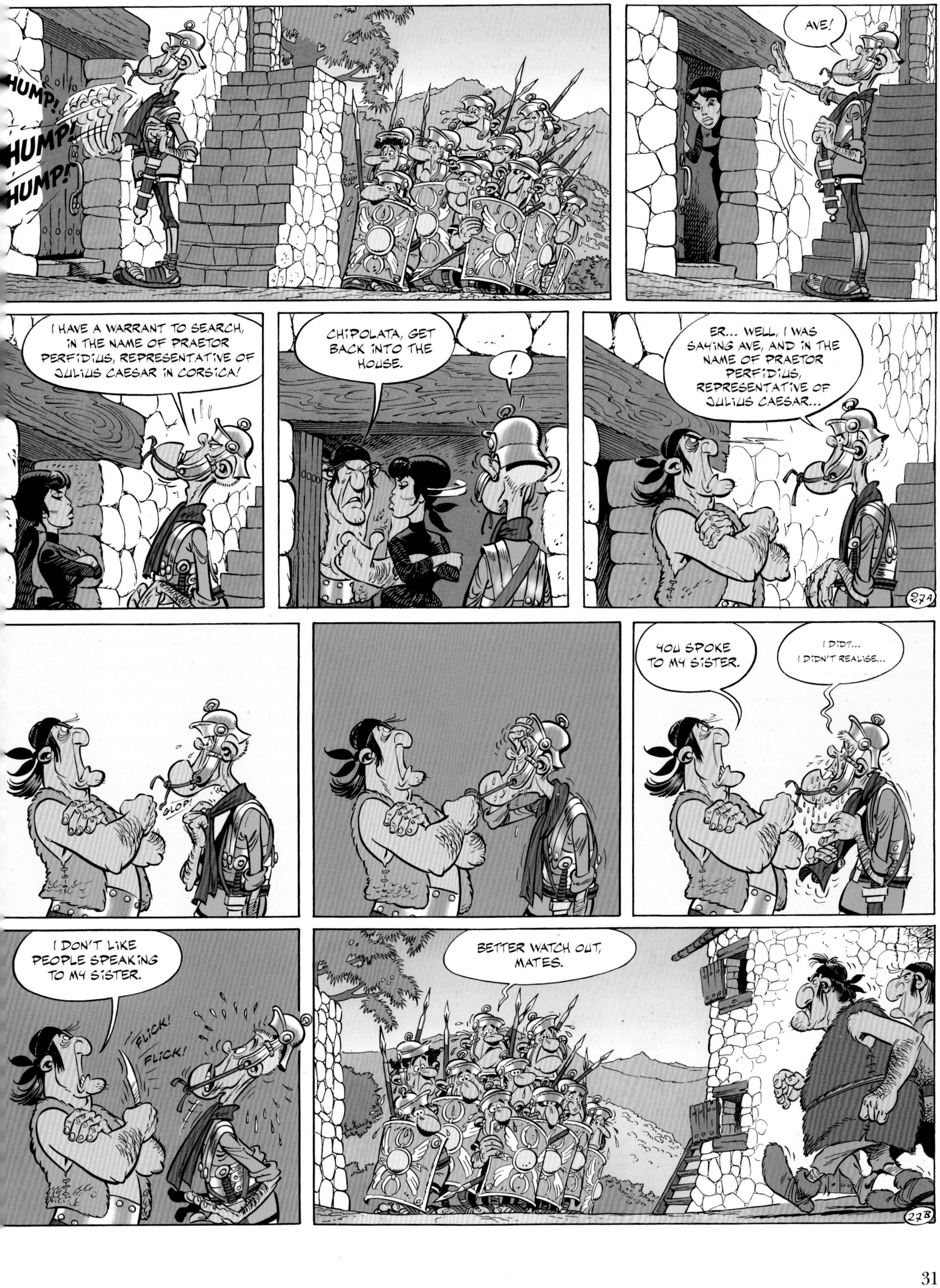

HUMP!
HUMP!
HUMP!
AVE!
I HAVE A WARRANT TO SEARCH, IN THE NAME OF PRAETOR PERFIDIUS, REPRESENTATIVE OF JULIUS CAESAR IN CORSICA!
CHIPOLATA, GET BACK INTO THE HOUSE.
!
ER... WELL, I WAS SAYING AVE, AND IN THE NAME OF PRAETOR PERFIDIUS, REPRESENTATIVE OF JULIUS CAESAR...
27A
GLOP!
YOU SPOKE TO MY SISTER.
I DID?... I DIDN'T REALISE...
I DON'T LIKE PEOPLE SPEAKING TO MY SISTER.
FLICK!
FLICK!
BETTER WATCH OUT, MATES.
27B

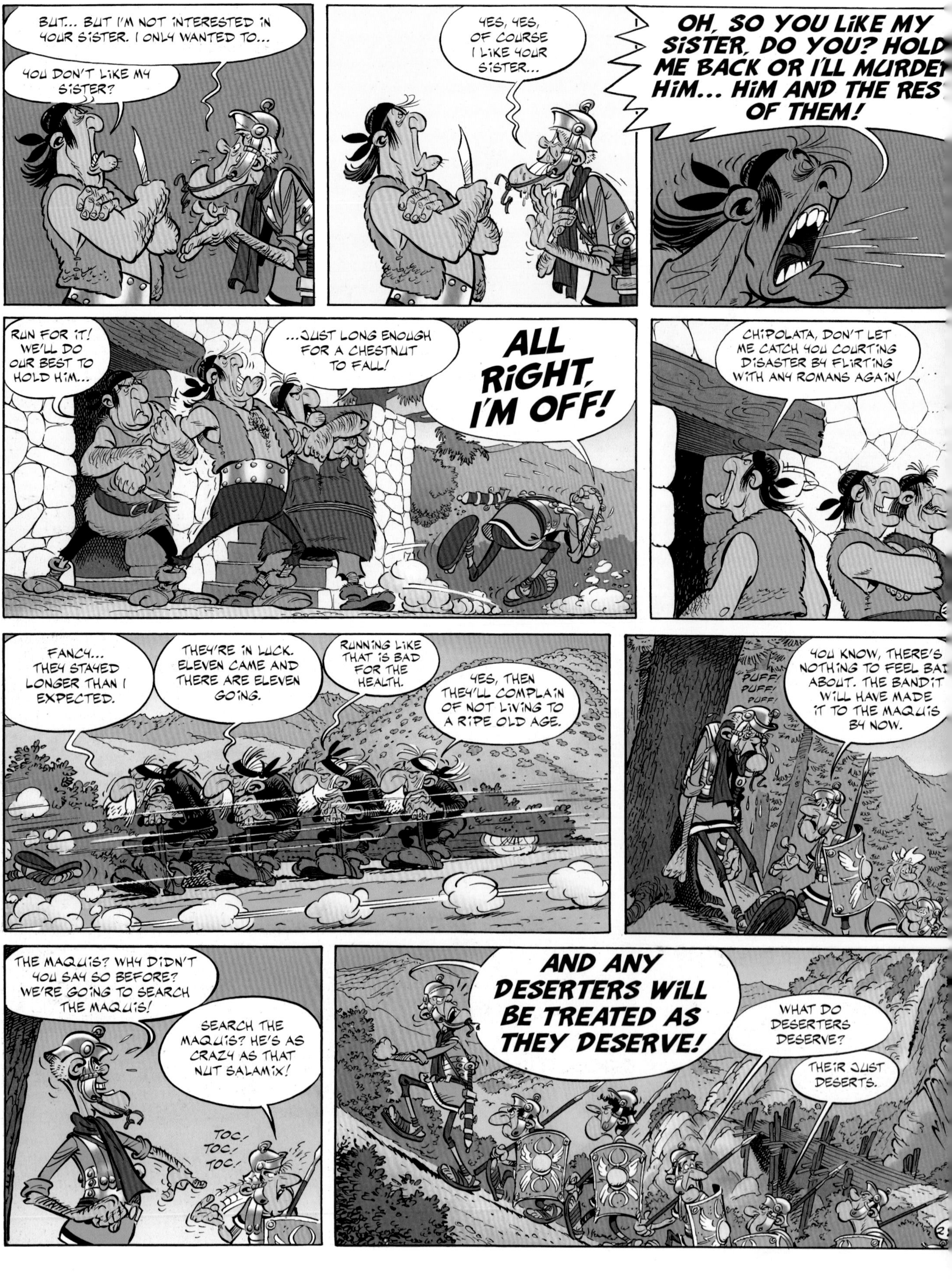
BUT... BUT I'M NOT INTERESTED IN YOUR SISTER. I ONLY WANTED TO...
YOU DON'T LIKE MY SISTER?
YES, YES, OF COURSE I LIKE YOUR SISTER...
OH, SO YOU LIKE MY SISTER, DO YOU? HOLD ME BACK OR I'LL MURDER HIM... HIM AND THE REST OF THEM!
RUN FOR IT! WE'LL DO OUR BEST TO HOLD HIM...
...JUST LONG ENOUGH FOR A CHESTNUT TO FALL!
ALL RIGHT, I'M OFF!
CHIPOLATA, DON'T LET ME CATCH YOU COURTING DISASTER BY FLIRTING WITH ANY ROMANS AGAIN!
FANCY... THEY STAYED LONGER THAN I EXPECTED.
THEY'RE IN LUCK. ELEVEN CAME AND THERE ARE ELEVEN GOING.
RUNNING LIKE THAT IS BAD FOR THE HEALTH.
YES, THEN THEY'LL COMPLAIN OF NOT LIVING TO A RIPE OLD AGE.
PUFF! PUFF! PUFF!
YOU KNOW, THERE'S NOTHING TO FEEL BAD ABOUT. THE BANDIT WILL HAVE MADE IT TO THE MAQUIS BY NOW.
THE MAQUIS? WHY DIDN'T YOU SAY SO BEFORE? WE'RE GOING TO SEARCH THE MAQUIS!
SEARCH THE MAQUIS? HE'S AS CRAZY AS THAT NUT SALAMIX!
TOC! TOC! TOC!
AND ANY DESERTERS WILL BE TREATED AS THEY DESERVE!
WHAT DO DESERTERS DESERVE?
THEIR JUST DESERTS.

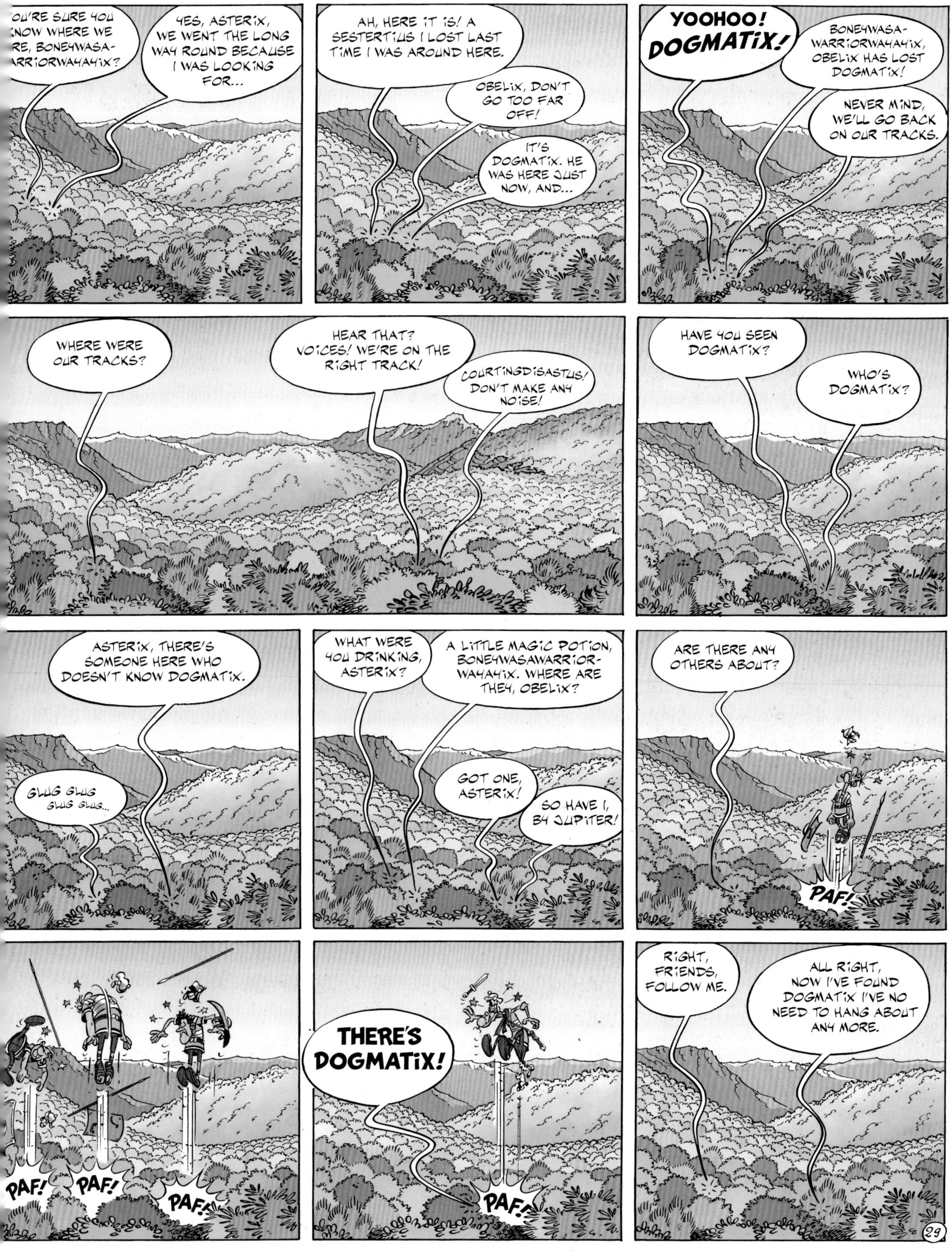
OU'RE SURE YOU
KNOW WHERE WE
RE, BONEYWASA-
ARRIORWAYAYIX?
YES, ASTERIX, WE WENT THE LONG WAY ROUND BECAUSE I WAS LOOKING FOR...
AH, HERE IT IS! A SESTERTIUS I LOST LAST TIME I WAS AROUND HERE.
OBELIX, DON'T GO TOO FAR OFF!
IT'S DOGMATIX. HE WAS HERE JUST NOW, AND...
YOOHOO! DOGMATIX!
BONEYWASA-WARRIORWAYAYIX, OBELIX HAS LOST DOGMATIX!
NEVER MIND, WE'LL GO BACK ON OUR TRACKS.
WHERE WERE OUR TRACKS?
HEAR THAT? VOICES! WE'RE ON THE RIGHT TRACK!
COURTINGDISASTUS! DON'T MAKE ANY NOISE!
HAVE YOU SEEN DOGMATIX?
WHO'S DOGMATIX?
ASTERIX, THERE'S SOMEONE HERE WHO DOESN'T KNOW DOGMATIX.
GLUG GLUG GLUG GLUG...
WHAT WERE YOU DRINKING, ASTERIX?
A LITTLE MAGIC POTION, BONEYWASAWARRIOR-WAYAYIX. WHERE ARE THEY, OBELIX?
GOT ONE, ASTERIX!
SO HAVE I, BY JUPITER!
ARE THERE ANY OTHERS ABOUT?
PAF!
PAF!
PAF!
PAF!
THERE'S DOGMATIX!
PAF!
RIGHT, FRIENDS, FOLLOW ME.
ALL RIGHT, NOW I'VE FOUND DOGMATIX I'VE NO NEED TO HANG ABOUT ANY MORE.
29

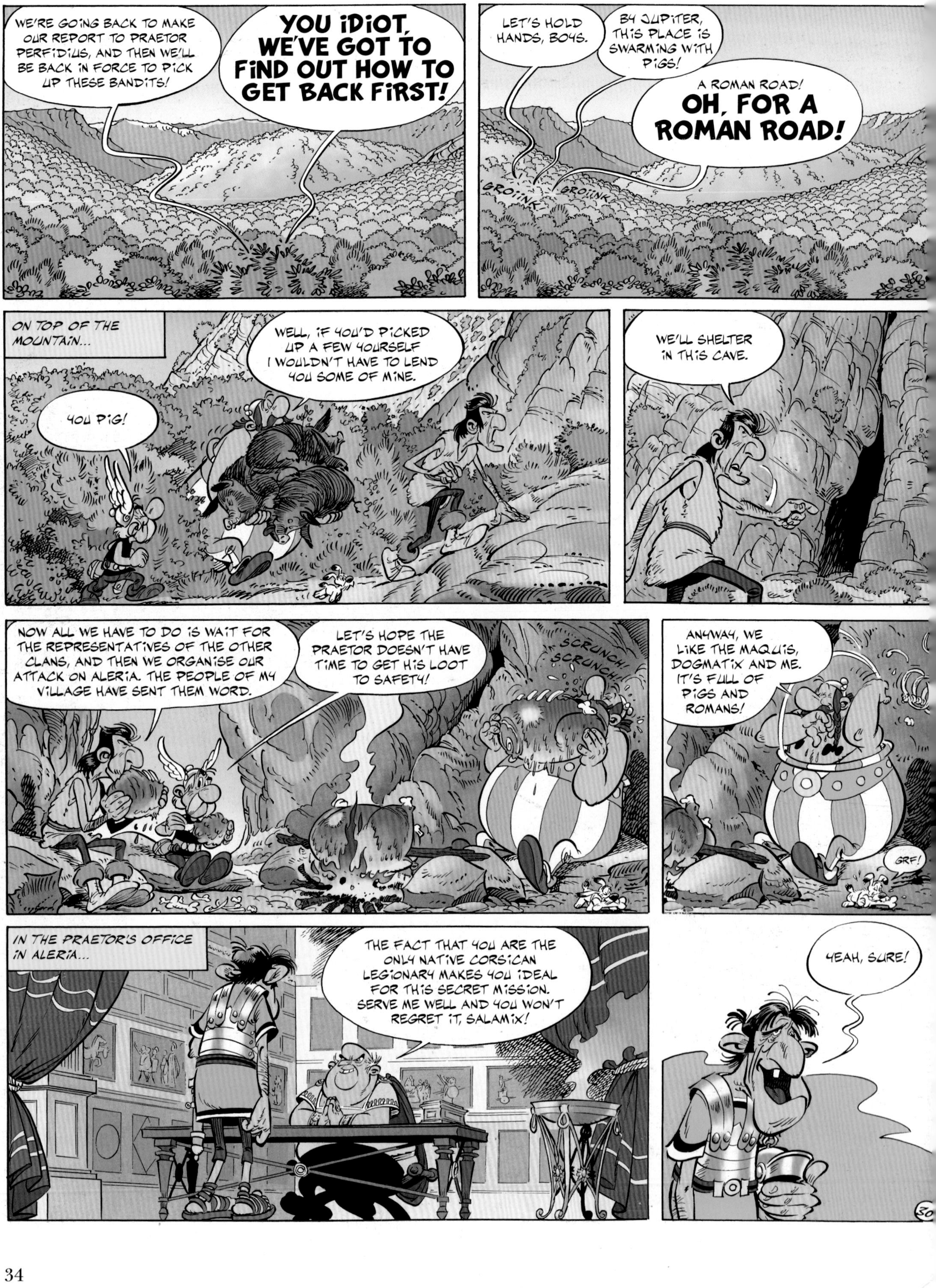
WE'RE GOING BACK TO MAKE OUR REPORT TO PRAETOR PERFIDIUS, AND THEN WE'LL BE BACK IN FORCE TO PICK UP THESE BANDITS!
YOU IDIOT, WE'VE GOT TO FIND OUT HOW TO GET BACK FIRST!
LET'S HOLD HANDS, BOYS.
BY JUPITER, THIS PLACE IS SWARMING WITH PIGS!
A ROMAN ROAD! OH, FOR A ROMAN ROAD!
GROÏNK
GROÏNK
ON TOP OF THE MOUNTAIN...
WELL, IF YOU'D PICKED UP A FEW YOURSELF I WOULDN'T HAVE TO LEND YOU SOME OF MINE.
YOU PIG!
WE'LL SHELTER IN THIS CAVE.
NOW ALL WE HAVE TO DO IS WAIT FOR THE REPRESENTATIVES OF THE OTHER CLANS, AND THEN WE ORGANISE OUR ATTACK ON ALERIA. THE PEOPLE OF MY VILLAGE HAVE SENT THEM WORD.
LET'S HOPE THE PRAETOR DOESN'T HAVE TIME TO GET HIS LOOT TO SAFETY!
SCRUNCH! SCRUNCH!
ANYWAY, WE LIKE THE MAQUIS, DOGMATIX AND ME. IT'S FULL OF PIGS AND ROMANS!
GRF!
IN THE PRAETOR'S OFFICE IN ALERIA...
THE FACT THAT YOU ARE THE ONLY NATIVE CORSICAN LEGIONARY MAKES YOU IDEAL FOR THIS SECRET MISSION. SERVE ME WELL AND YOU WON'T REGRET IT, SALAMIX!
YEAH, SURE!
30

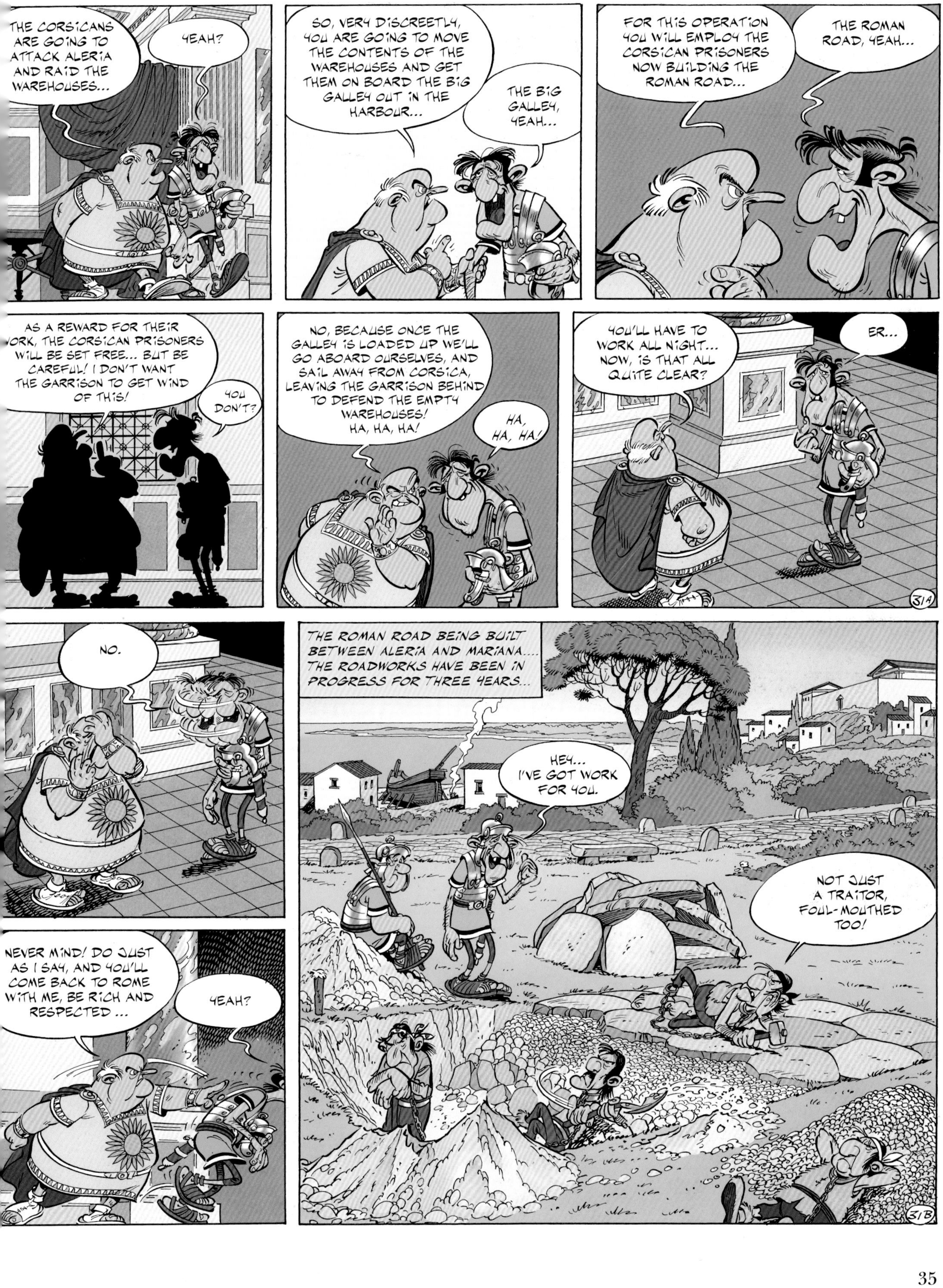
THE CORSICANS ARE GOING TO ATTACK ALERIA AND RAID THE WAREHOUSES...
YEAH?
SO, VERY DISCREETLY, YOU ARE GOING TO MOVE THE CONTENTS OF THE WAREHOUSES AND GET THEM ON BOARD THE BIG GALLEY OUT IN THE HARBOUR...
THE BIG GALLEY, YEAH...
FOR THIS OPERATION YOU WILL EMPLOY THE CORSICAN PRISONERS NOW BUILDING THE ROMAN ROAD...
THE ROMAN ROAD, YEAH...
AS A REWARD FOR THEIR WORK, THE CORSICAN PRISONERS WILL BE SET FREE... BUT BE CAREFUL! I DON'T WANT THE GARRISON TO GET WIND OF THIS!
YOU DON'T?
NO, BECAUSE ONCE THE GALLEY IS LOADED UP WE'LL GO ABOARD OURSELVES, AND SAIL AWAY FROM CORSICA, LEAVING THE GARRISON BEHIND TO DEFEND THE EMPTY WAREHOUSES! HA, HA, HA!
HA, HA, HA!
YOU'LL HAVE TO WORK ALL NIGHT... NOW, IS THAT ALL QUITE CLEAR?
ER...
31A
NO.
NEVER MIND! DO JUST AS I SAY, AND YOU'LL COME BACK TO ROME WITH ME, BE RICH AND RESPECTED ...
YEAH?
THE ROMAN ROAD BEING BUILT BETWEEN ALERIA AND MARIANA.... THE ROADWORKS HAVE BEEN IN PROGRESS FOR THREE YEARS...
HEY... I'VE GOT WORK FOR YOU.
NOT JUST A TRAITOR, FOUL-MOUTHED TOO!
31B

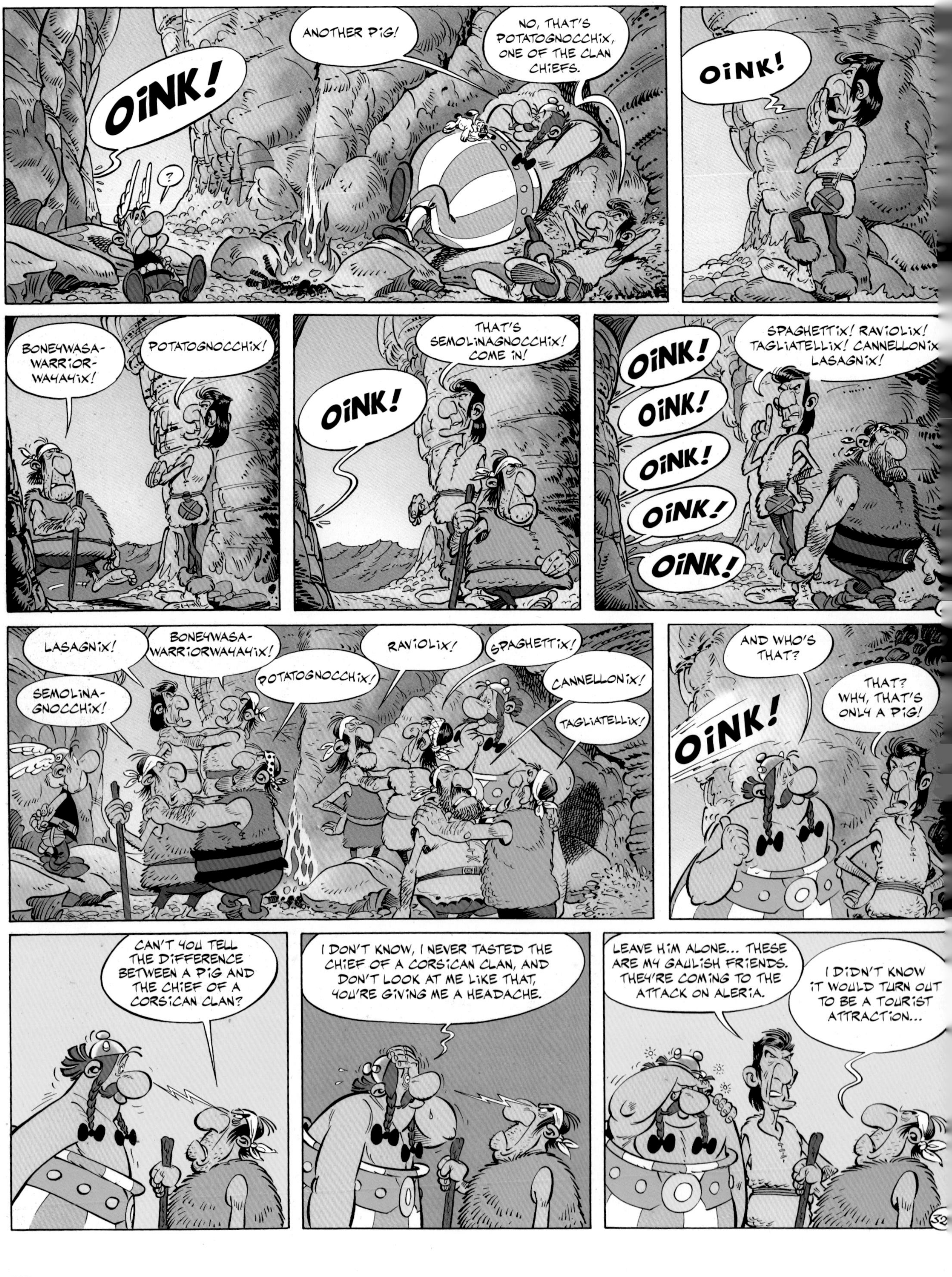
OINK!
?
ANOTHER PIG!
NO, THAT'S POTATOGNOCCHIX, ONE OF THE CLAN CHIEFS.
OINK!
BONEYWASA-WARRIOR-WAYAYIX!
POTATOGNOCCHIX!
OINK!
THAT'S SEMOLINAGNOCCHIX! COME IN!
OINK!
OINK!
OINK!
OINK!
OINK!
SPAGHETTIX! RAVIOLIX! TAGLIATELLIX! CANNELLONIX LASAGNIX!
LASAGNIX!
BONEYWASA-WARRIORWAYAYIX!
SEMOLINA-GNOCCHIX!
POTATOGNOCCHIX!
RAVIOLIX!
SPAGHETTIX!
CANNELLONIX!
TAGLIATELLIX!
AND WHO'S THAT?
OINK!
THAT? WHY, THAT'S ONLY A PIG!
CAN'T YOU TELL THE DIFFERENCE BETWEEN A PIG AND THE CHIEF OF A CORSICAN CLAN?
I DON'T KNOW, I NEVER TASTED THE CHIEF OF A CORSICAN CLAN, AND DON'T LOOK AT ME LIKE THAT, YOU'RE GIVING ME A HEADACHE.
LEAVE HIM ALONE... THESE ARE MY GAULISH FRIENDS. THEY'RE COMING TO THE ATTACK ON ALERIA.
I DIDN'T KNOW IT WOULD TURN OUT TO BE A TOURIST ATTRACTION...

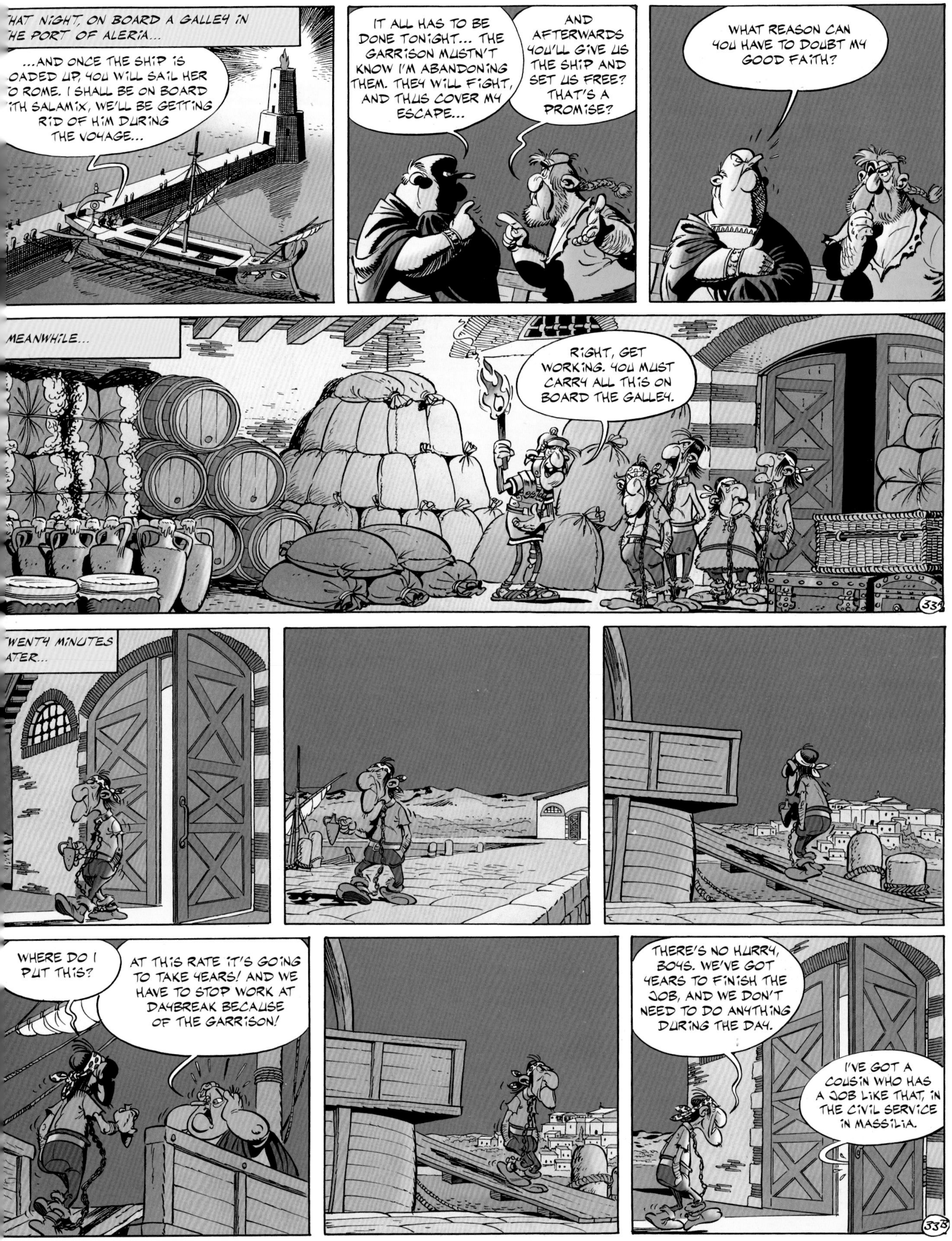

HAT NIGHT, ON BOARD A GALLEY IN HE PORT OF ALERIA...
...AND ONCE THE SHIP IS OADED UP, YOU WILL SAIL HER O ROME. I SHALL BE ON BOARD ITH SALAMIX, WE'LL BE GETTING RID OF HIM DURING THE VOYAGE...
IT ALL HAS TO BE DONE TONIGHT... THE GARRISON MUSTN'T KNOW I'M ABANDONING THEM. THEY WILL FIGHT, AND THUS COVER MY ESCAPE...
AND AFTERWARDS YOU'LL GIVE US THE SHIP AND SET US FREE? THAT'S A PROMISE?
WHAT REASON CAN YOU HAVE TO DOUBT MY GOOD FAITH?
MEANWHILE...
RIGHT, GET WORKING. YOU MUST CARRY ALL THIS ON BOARD THE GALLEY.
WENTY MINUTES ATER...
WHERE DO I PUT THIS?
AT THIS RATE IT'S GOING TO TAKE YEARS! AND WE HAVE TO STOP WORK AT DAYBREAK BECAUSE OF THE GARRISON!
THERE'S NO HURRY, BOYS. WE'VE GOT YEARS TO FINISH THE JOB, AND WE DON'T NEED TO DO ANYTHING DURING THE DAY.
I'VE GOT A COUSIN WHO HAS A JOB LIKE THAT, IN THE CIVIL SERVICE IN MASSILIA.

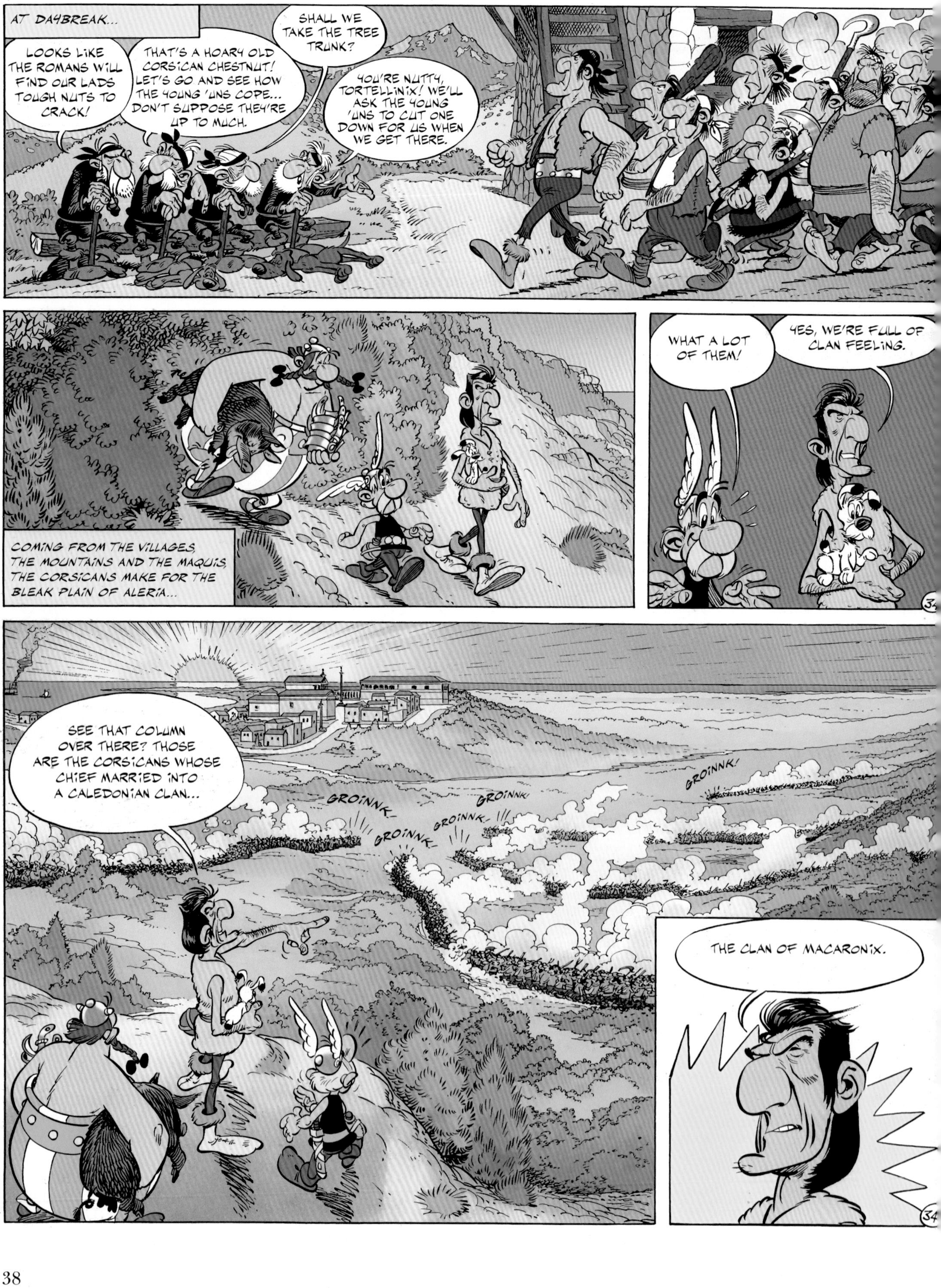
AT DAYBREAK...
LOOKS LIKE THE ROMANS WILL FIND OUR LADS TOUGH NUTS TO CRACK!
THAT'S A HOARY OLD CORSICAN CHESTNUT! LET'S GO AND SEE HOW THE YOUNG 'UNS COPE... DON'T SUPPOSE THEY'RE UP TO MUCH.
SHALL WE TAKE THE TREE TRUNK?
YOU'RE NUTTY, TORTELLINIX! WE'LL ASK THE YOUNG 'UNS TO CUT ONE DOWN FOR US WHEN WE GET THERE.
COMING FROM THE VILLAGES, THE MOUNTAINS AND THE MAQUIS, THE CORSICANS MAKE FOR THE BLEAK PLAIN OF ALERIA...
WHAT A LOT OF THEM!
YES, WE'RE FULL OF CLAN FEELING.
SEE THAT COLUMN OVER THERE? THOSE ARE THE CORSICANS WHOSE CHIEF MARRIED INTO A CALEDONIAN CLAN...
GROINNK!
GROINNK
GROINNK!
GROINNK
GROINNK
THE CLAN OF MACARONIX.

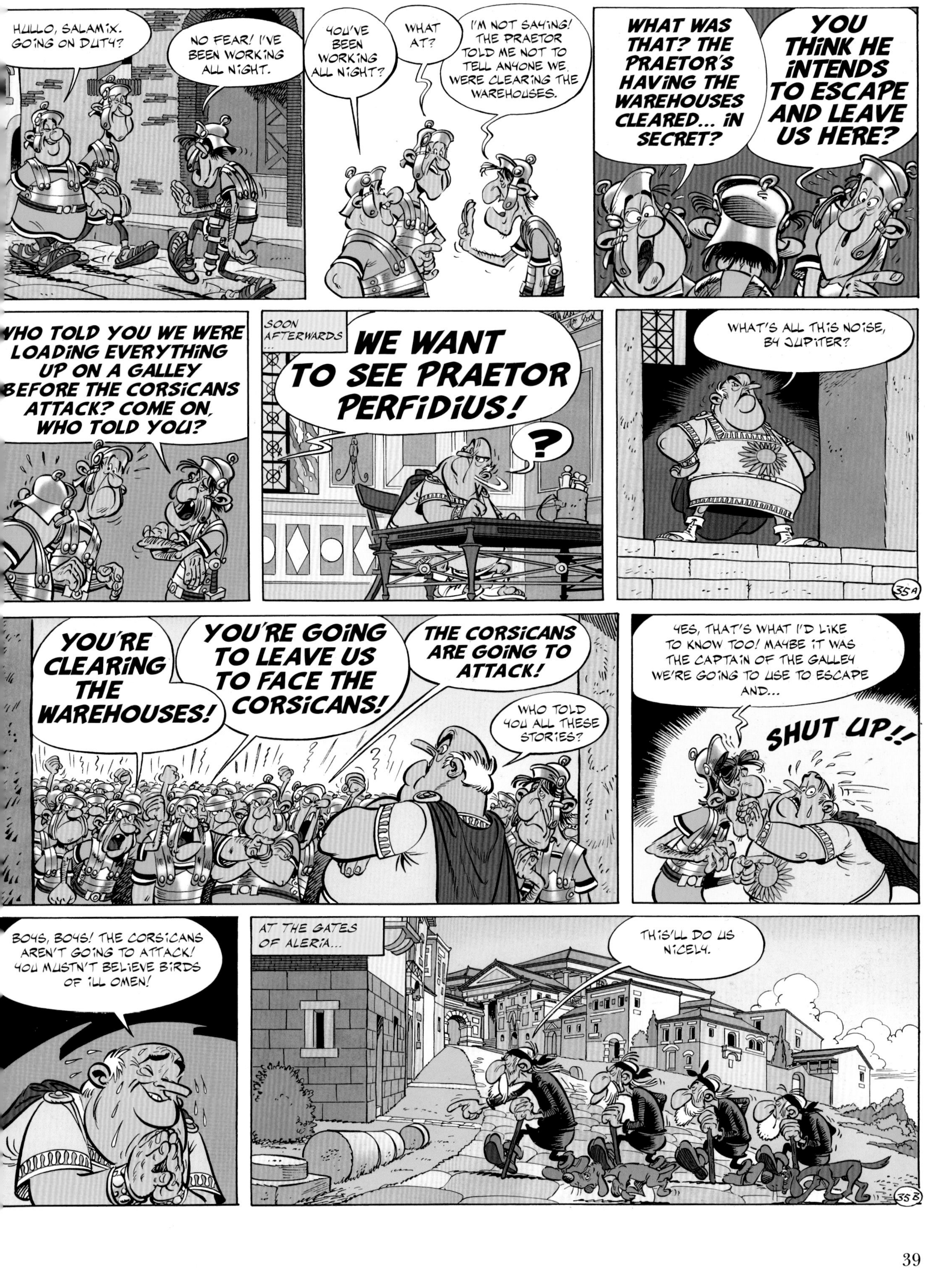
HULLO, SALAMIX. GOING ON DUTY?
NO FEAR! I'VE BEEN WORKING ALL NIGHT.
YOU'VE BEEN WORKING ALL NIGHT?
WHAT AT?
I'M NOT SAYING! THE PRAETOR TOLD ME NOT TO TELL ANYONE WE WERE CLEARING THE WAREHOUSES.
WHAT WAS THAT? THE PRAETOR'S HAVING THE WAREHOUSES CLEARED... IN SECRET?
YOU THINK HE INTENDS TO ESCAPE AND LEAVE US HERE?
WHO TOLD YOU WE WERE LOADING EVERYTHING UP ON A GALLEY BEFORE THE CORSICANS ATTACK? COME ON, WHO TOLD YOU?
SOON AFTERWARDS ...
WE WANT TO SEE PRAETOR PERFIDIUS!
?
WHAT'S ALL THIS NOISE, BY JUPITER?
35A
YOU'RE CLEARING THE WAREHOUSES!
YOU'RE GOING TO LEAVE US TO FACE THE CORSICANS!
THE CORSICANS ARE GOING TO ATTACK!
WHO TOLD YOU ALL THESE STORIES?
YES, THAT'S WHAT I'D LIKE TO KNOW TOO! MAYBE IT WAS THE CAPTAIN OF THE GALLEY WE'RE GOING TO USE TO ESCAPE AND...
SHUT UP!!
BOYS, BOYS! THE CORSICANS AREN'T GOING TO ATTACK! YOU MUSTN'T BELIEVE BIRDS OF ILL OMEN!
AT THE GATES OF ALERIA...
THIS'LL DO US NICELY.
35B

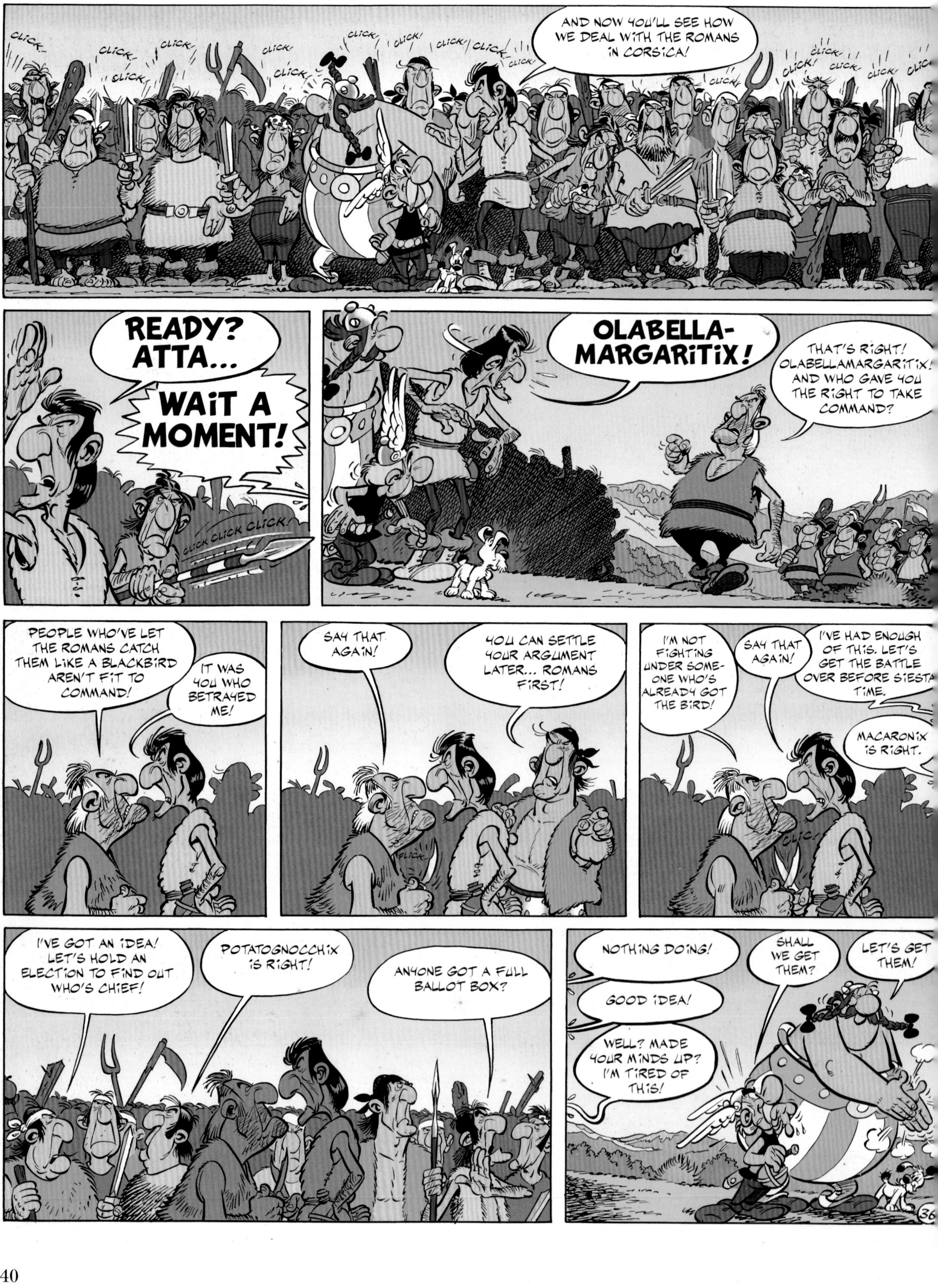
CLICK
CLICK
CLICK
CLICK
CLICK
CLICK!
CLICK!
CLICK
CLICK!
AND NOW YOU'LL SEE HOW WE DEAL WITH THE ROMANS IN CORSICA!
CLICK
CLICK!
CLICK
CLICK!
READY? ATTA...
WAIT A MOMENT!
CLICK CLICK CLICK!
OLABELLA-MARGARITIX!
THAT'S RIGHT! OLABELLAMARGARITIX! AND WHO GAVE YOU THE RIGHT TO TAKE COMMAND?
PEOPLE WHO'VE LET THE ROMANS CATCH THEM LIKE A BLACKBIRD AREN'T FIT TO COMMAND!
IT WAS YOU WHO BETRAYED ME!
SAY THAT AGAIN!
YOU CAN SETTLE YOUR ARGUMENT LATER... ROMANS FIRST!
FLICK
I'M NOT FIGHTING UNDER SOMEONE WHO'S ALREADY GOT THE BIRD!
SAY THAT AGAIN!
I'VE HAD ENOUGH OF THIS. LET'S GET THE BATTLE OVER BEFORE SIESTA TIME.
MACARONIX IS RIGHT.
CLIC!
I'VE GOT AN IDEA! LET'S HOLD AN ELECTION TO FIND OUT WHO'S CHIEF!
POTATOGNOCCHIX IS RIGHT!
ANYONE GOT A FULL BALLOT BOX?
NOTHING DOING!
GOOD IDEA!
WELL? MADE YOUR MINDS UP? I'M TIRED OF THIS!
SHALL WE GET THEM?
LET'S GET THEM!
36

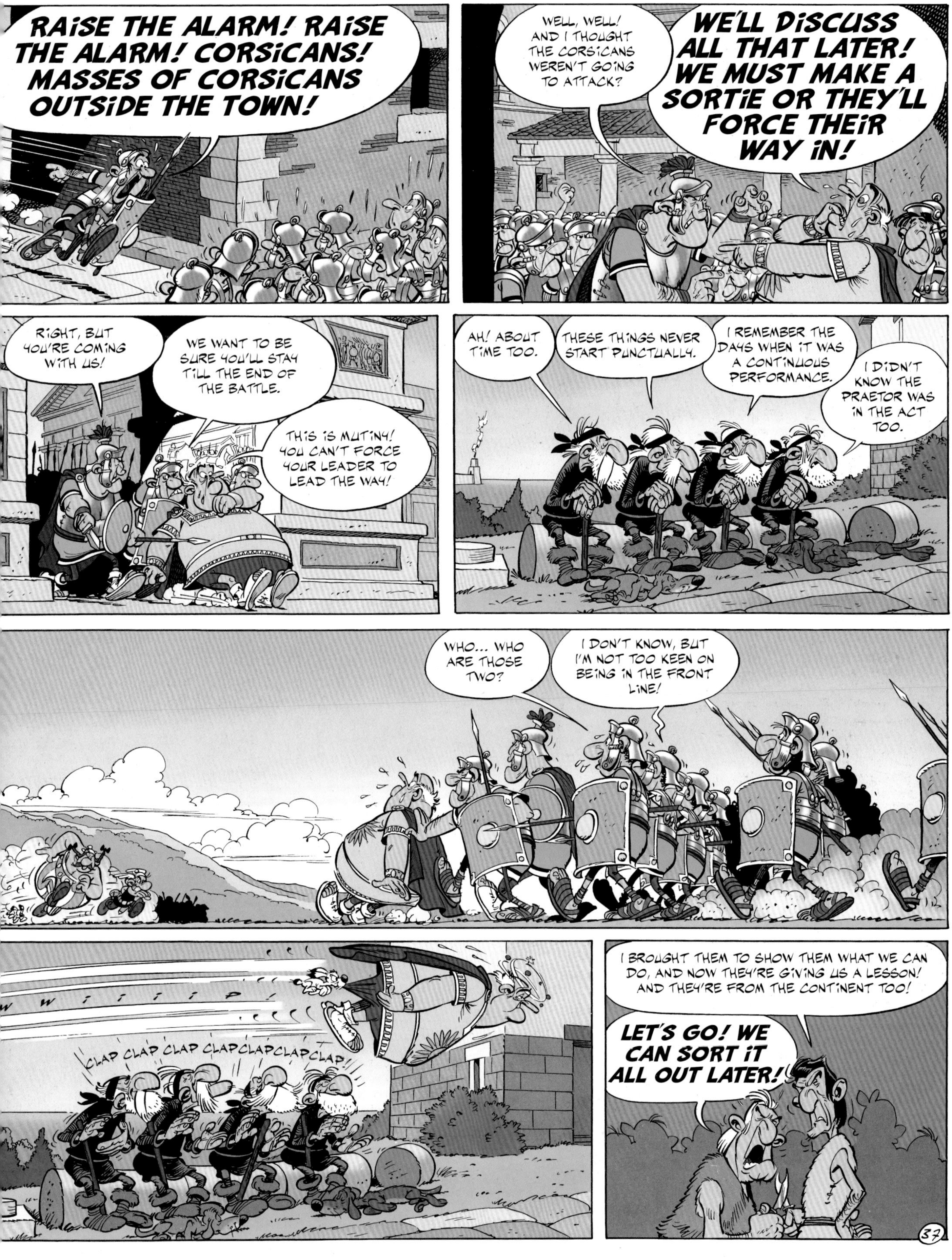
RAISE THE ALARM! RAISE THE ALARM! CORSICANS! MASSES OF CORSICANS OUTSIDE THE TOWN!
WELL, WELL! AND I THOUGHT THE CORSICANS WEREN'T GOING TO ATTACK?
WE'LL DISCUSS ALL THAT LATER! WE MUST MAKE A SORTIE OR THEY'LL FORCE THEIR WAY IN!
RIGHT, BUT YOU'RE COMING WITH US!
WE WANT TO BE SURE YOU'LL STAY TILL THE END OF THE BATTLE.
THIS IS MUTINY! YOU CAN'T FORCE YOUR LEADER TO LEAD THE WAY!
AH! ABOUT TIME TOO.
THESE THINGS NEVER START PUNCTUALLY.
I REMEMBER THE DAYS WHEN IT WAS A CONTINUOUS PERFORMANCE.
I DIDN'T KNOW THE PRAETOR WAS IN THE ACT TOO.
WHO... WHO ARE THOSE TWO?
I DON'T KNOW, BUT I'M NOT TOO KEEN ON BEING IN THE FRONT LINE!
CLAP CLAP CLAP CLAPCLAPCLAPCLAP
I BROUGHT THEM TO SHOW THEM WHAT WE CAN DO, AND NOW THEY'RE GIVING US A LESSON! AND THEY'RE FROM THE CONTINENT TOO!
LET'S GO! WE CAN SORT IT ALL OUT LATER!
37

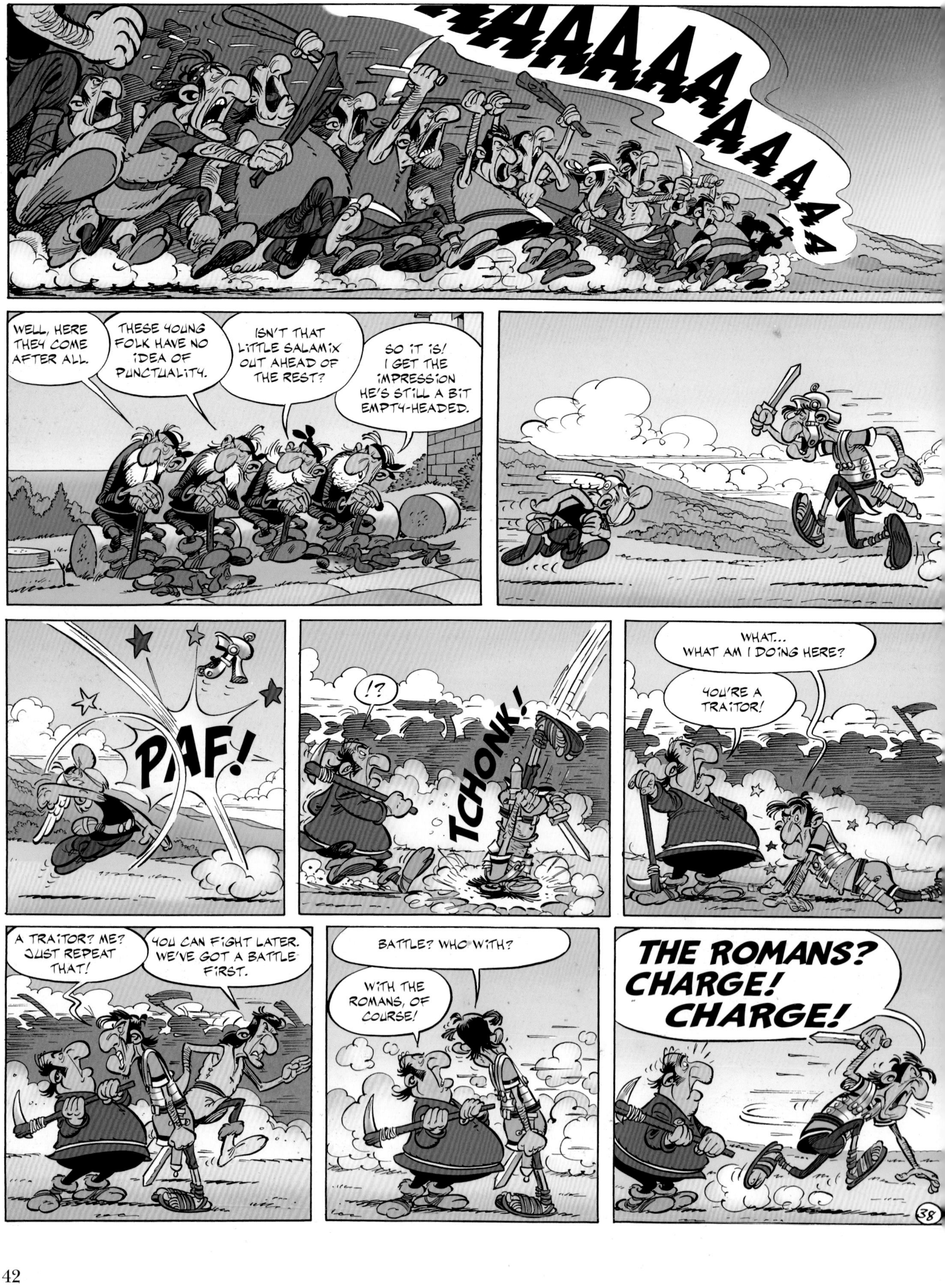
AAAAAAAAAAAAAA
WELL, HERE THEY COME AFTER ALL.
THESE YOUNG FOLK HAVE NO IDEA OF PUNCTUALITY.
ISN'T THAT LITTLE SALAMIX OUT AHEAD OF THE REST?
SO IT IS! I GET THE IMPRESSION HE'S STILL A BIT EMPTY-HEADED.
PAF!
!?
TCHONK!
WHAT... WHAT AM I DOING HERE?
YOU'RE A TRAITOR!
A TRAITOR? ME? JUST REPEAT THAT!
YOU CAN FIGHT LATER. WE'VE GOT A BATTLE FIRST.
BATTLE? WHO WITH?
WITH THE ROMANS, OF COURSE!
THE ROMANS? CHARGE! CHARGE!
38

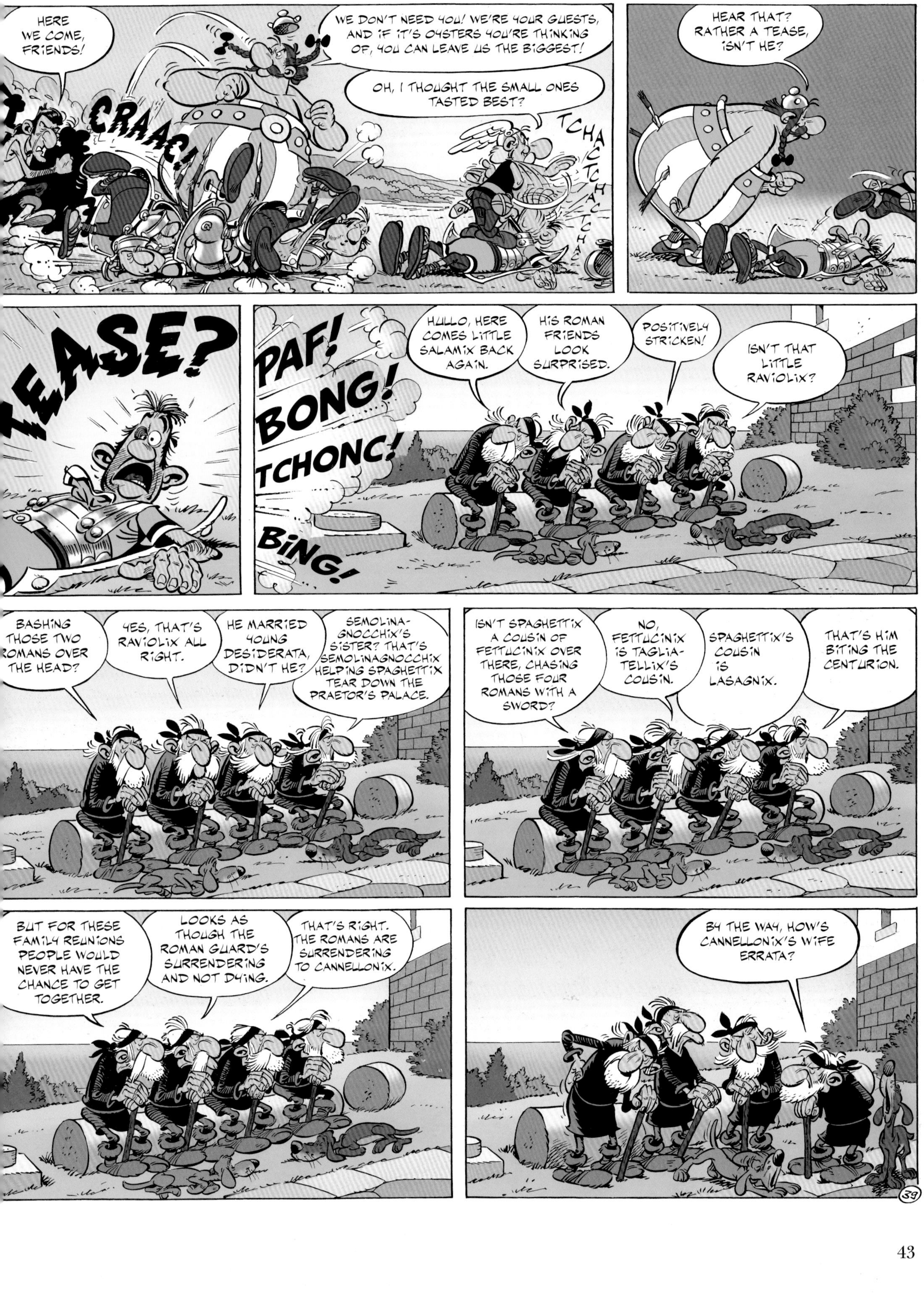
HERE WE COME, FRIENDS!
CRAAC!
WE DON'T NEED YOU! WE'RE YOUR GUESTS, AND IF IT'S OYSTERS YOU'RE THINKING OF, YOU CAN LEAVE US THE BIGGEST!
OH, I THOUGHT THE SMALL ONES TASTED BEST?
TCHACTCHACTCHAC
HEAR THAT? RATHER A TEASE, ISN'T HE?
TEASE?
PAF!
BONG!
TCHONC!
BING!
HULLO, HERE COMES LITTLE SALAMIX BACK AGAIN.
HIS ROMAN FRIENDS LOOK SURPRISED.
POSITIVELY STRICKEN!
ISN'T THAT LITTLE RAVIOLIX?
BASHING THOSE TWO ROMANS OVER THE HEAD?
YES, THAT'S RAVIOLIX ALL RIGHT.
HE MARRIED YOUNG DESIDERATA, DIDN'T HE?
SEMOLINA-GNOCCHIX'S SISTER? THAT'S SEMOLINAGNOCCHIX HELPING SPAGHETTIX TEAR DOWN THE PRAETOR'S PALACE.
ISN'T SPAGHETTIX A COUSIN OF FETTUCINIX OVER THERE, CHASING THOSE FOUR ROMANS WITH A SWORD?
NO, FETTUCINIX IS TAGLIA-TELLIX'S COUSIN.
SPAGHETTIX'S COUSIN IS LASAGNIX.
THAT'S HIM BITING THE CENTURION.
BUT FOR THESE FAMILY REUNIONS PEOPLE WOULD NEVER HAVE THE CHANCE TO GET TOGETHER.
LOOKS AS THOUGH THE ROMAN GUARD'S SURRENDERING AND NOT DYING.
THAT'S RIGHT. THE ROMANS ARE SURRENDERING TO CANNELLONIX.
BY THE WAY, HOW'S CANNELLONIX'S WIFE ERRATA?
39

LOST SOMETHING?
PRAETOR PERFIDIUS. I'VE GOT A WORD OR SO TO SAY TO HIM.
I KNOW WHERE HE IS! I REMEMBER NOW... HE WAS GOING TO ESCAPE, ON BOARD A SHIP!
SHOW US THE WAY. WE'LL BRING HIM BACK. OBELIX WILL COME TOO.
OOH, YES! WE'RE VERY GOOD ON SHIPS!
MEANWHILE, ON BOARD THE SHIP...
...AND THEN, DURING THE VOYAGE, WE'LL THROW THE ROMAN OVERBOARD AND SAIL OFF WITH THE LOOT!
CAST OFF! CAST OFF!
HE'LL GET A STITCH THAT WAY... DO WE CAST OFF?
GO SLOW...
QUICK! QUICK! CAST OFF!
A BIT OF PLAIN DEALING FIRST. WHERE'S THE LOOT YOU'VE PURLOINED? WE'VE ONLY GOT ONE AMPHORA ON BOARD SO FAR.
CAP'N! LOOK!
THE GAU... THE GAUGAU...
CAST OFF! QUICK! CAST OFF!!!
THAT'S JUST WHAT I WAS SAYING! CAST OFF!
40

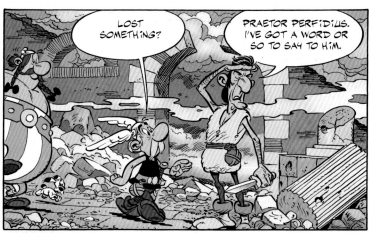

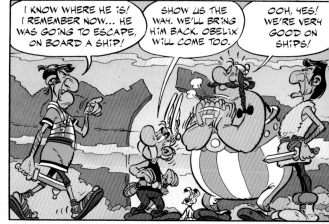

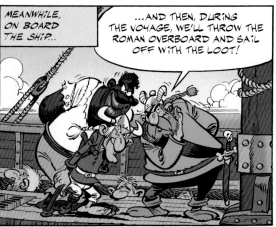

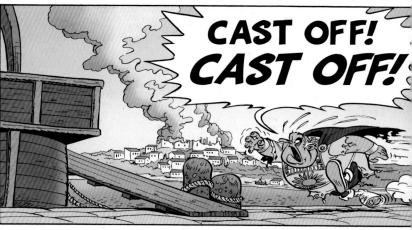

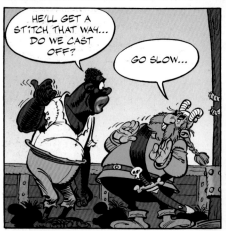

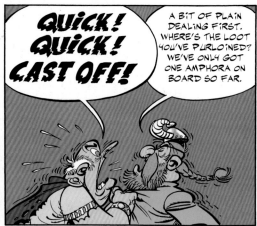

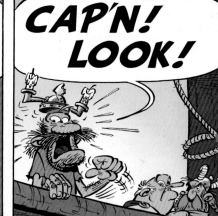

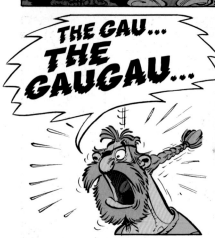

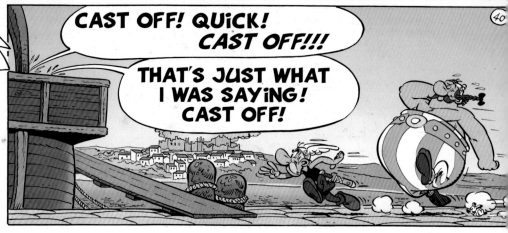

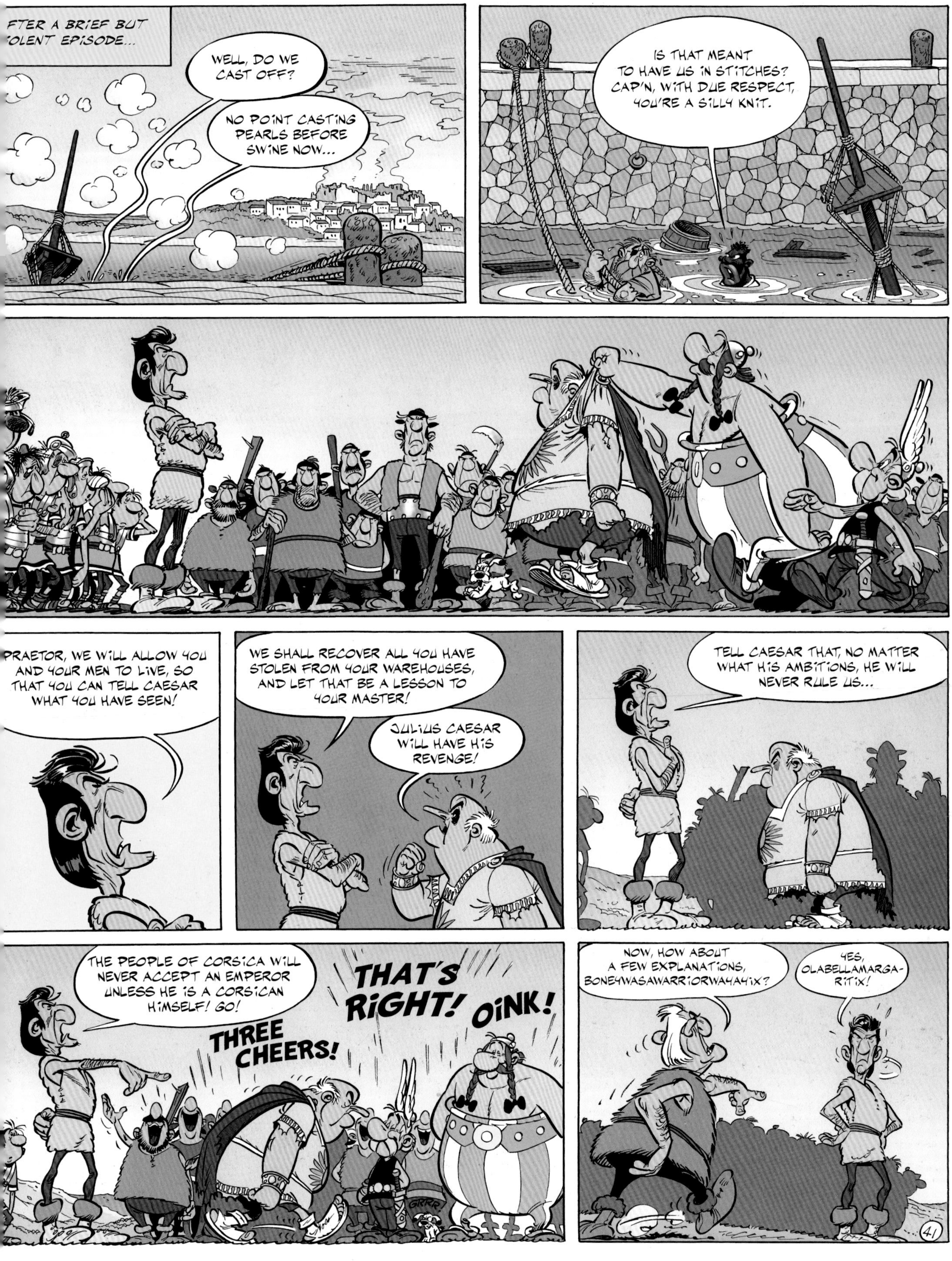
FTER A BRIEF BUT
OLENT EPISODE...
WELL, DO WE CAST OFF?
NO POINT CASTING PEARLS BEFORE SWINE NOW...
IS THAT MEANT TO HAVE US IN STITCHES? CAP'N, WITH DUE RESPECT, YOU'RE A SILLY KNIT.
PRAETOR, WE WILL ALLOW YOU AND YOUR MEN TO LIVE, SO THAT YOU CAN TELL CAESAR WHAT YOU HAVE SEEN!
WE SHALL RECOVER ALL YOU HAVE STOLEN FROM YOUR WAREHOUSES, AND LET THAT BE A LESSON TO YOUR MASTER!
JULIUS CAESAR WILL HAVE HIS REVENGE!
TELL CAESAR THAT, NO MATTER WHAT HIS AMBITIONS, HE WILL NEVER RULE US...
THE PEOPLE OF CORSICA WILL NEVER ACCEPT AN EMPEROR UNLESS HE IS A CORSICAN HIMSELF! GO!
THREE CHEERS!
THAT'S RIGHT!
OINK!
GRRR
NOW, HOW ABOUT A FEW EXPLANATIONS, BONEYWASAWARRIORWAYAYIX?
YES, OLABELLAMARGA-RITIX!
41

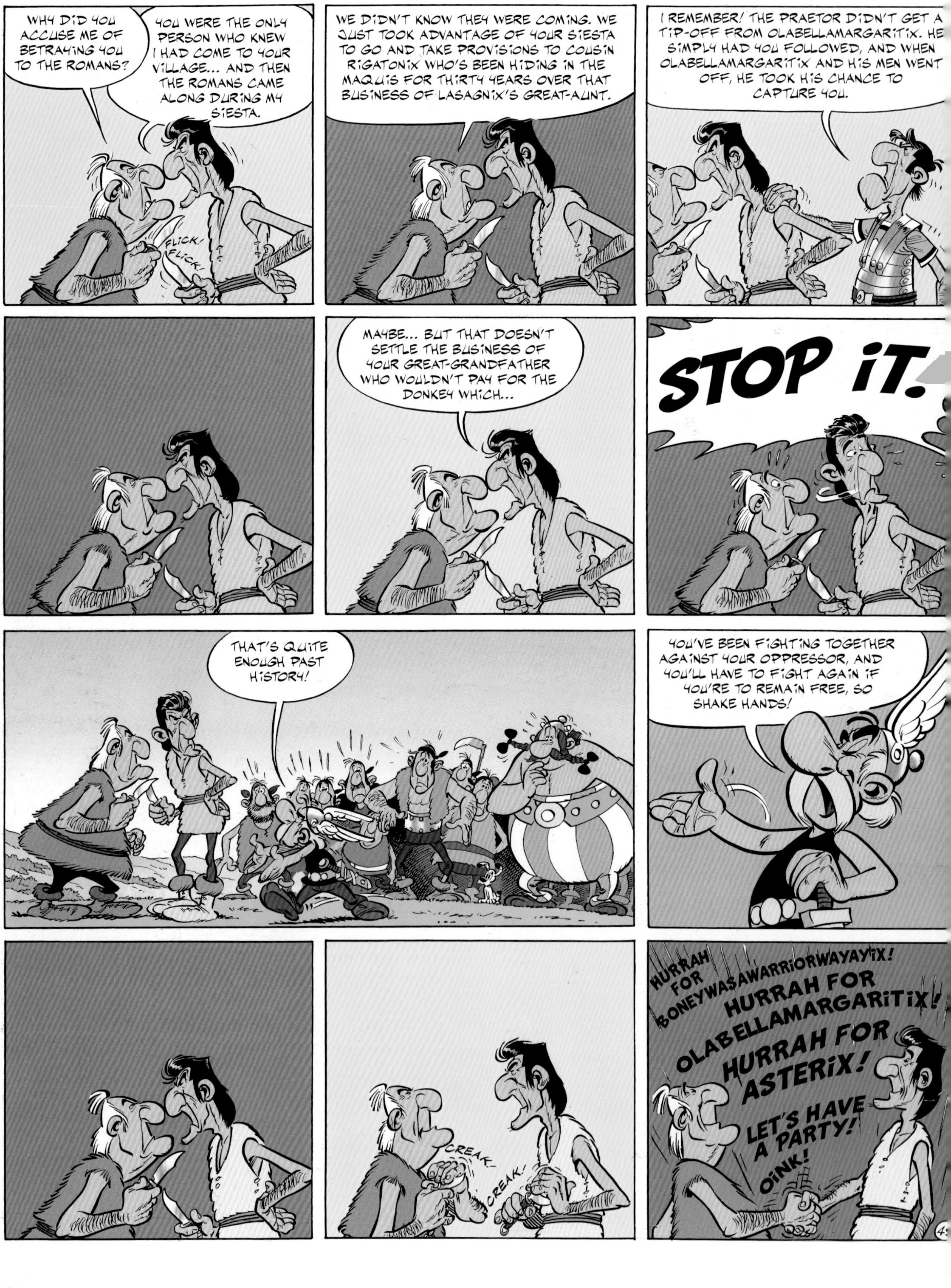
WHY DID YOU ACCUSE ME OF BETRAYING YOU TO THE ROMANS?
YOU WERE THE ONLY PERSON WHO KNEW I HAD COME TO YOUR VILLAGE... AND THEN THE ROMANS CAME ALONG DURING MY SIESTA.
FLICK! FLICK!
WE DIDN'T KNOW THEY WERE COMING. WE JUST TOOK ADVANTAGE OF YOUR SIESTA TO GO AND TAKE PROVISIONS TO COUSIN RIGATONIX WHO'S BEEN HIDING IN THE MAQUIS FOR THIRTY YEARS OVER THAT BUSINESS OF LASAGNIX'S GREAT-AUNT.
I REMEMBER! THE PRAETOR DIDN'T GET A TIP-OFF FROM OLABELLAMARGARITIX. HE SIMPLY HAD YOU FOLLOWED, AND WHEN OLABELLAMARGARITIX AND HIS MEN WENT OFF, HE TOOK HIS CHANCE TO CAPTURE YOU.
MAYBE... BUT THAT DOESN'T SETTLE THE BUSINESS OF YOUR GREAT-GRANDFATHER WHO WOULDN'T PAY FOR THE DONKEY WHICH...
STOP IT.
THAT'S QUITE ENOUGH PAST HISTORY!
YOU'VE BEEN FIGHTING TOGETHER AGAINST YOUR OPPRESSOR, AND YOU'LL HAVE TO FIGHT AGAIN IF YOU'RE TO REMAIN FREE, SO SHAKE HANDS!
CREAK-
CREAK!
HURRAH FOR BONEYWASAWARRIORWAYAYIX!
HURRAH FOR OLABELLAMARGARITIX!
HURRAH FOR ASTERIX!
LET'S HAVE A PARTY!
OINK!

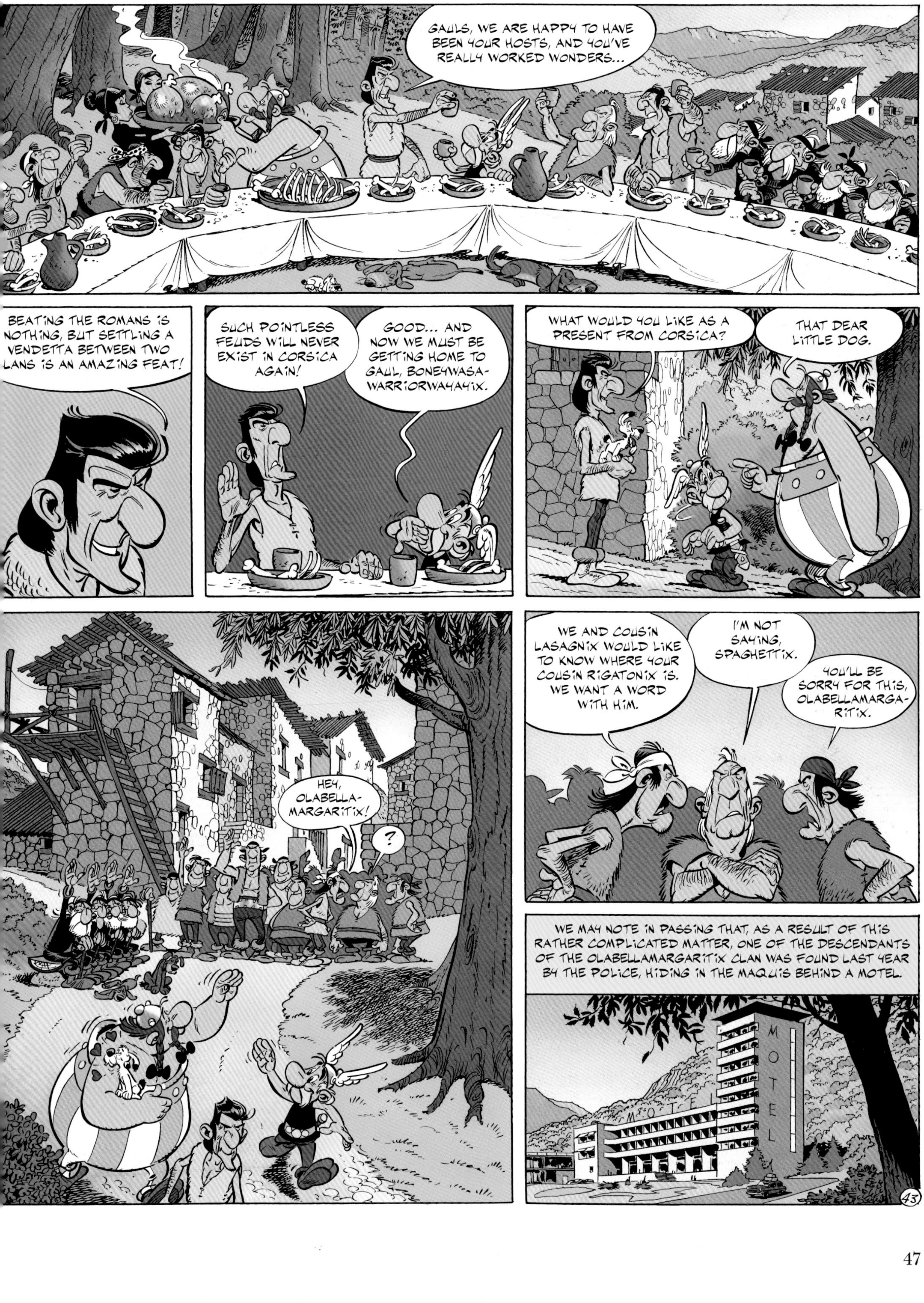
GAULS, WE ARE HAPPY TO HAVE BEEN YOUR HOSTS, AND YOU'VE REALLY WORKED WONDERS...
BEATING THE ROMANS IS NOTHING, BUT SETTLING A VENDETTA BETWEEN TWO LANS IS AN AMAZING FEAT!
SUCH POINTLESS FEUDS WILL NEVER EXIST IN CORSICA AGAIN!
GOOD... AND NOW WE MUST BE GETTING HOME TO GAUL, BONEYWASAWARRIORWAYAYIX.
WHAT WOULD YOU LIKE AS A PRESENT FROM CORSICA?
THAT DEAR LITTLE DOG.
HEY, OLABELLAMARGARITIX!
?
WE AND COUSIN LASAGNIX WOULD LIKE TO KNOW WHERE YOUR COUSIN RIGATONIX IS. WE WANT A WORD WITH HIM.
I'M NOT SAYING, SPAGHETTIX.
YOU'LL BE SORRY FOR THIS, OLABELLAMARGARITIX.
WE MAY NOTE IN PASSING THAT, AS A RESULT OF THIS RATHER COMPLICATED MATTER, ONE OF THE DESCENDANTS OF THE OLABELLAMARGARITIX CLAN WAS FOUND LAST YEAR BY THE POLICE, HIDING IN THE MAQUIS BEHIND A MOTEL.
MOTEL
MOTEL
43

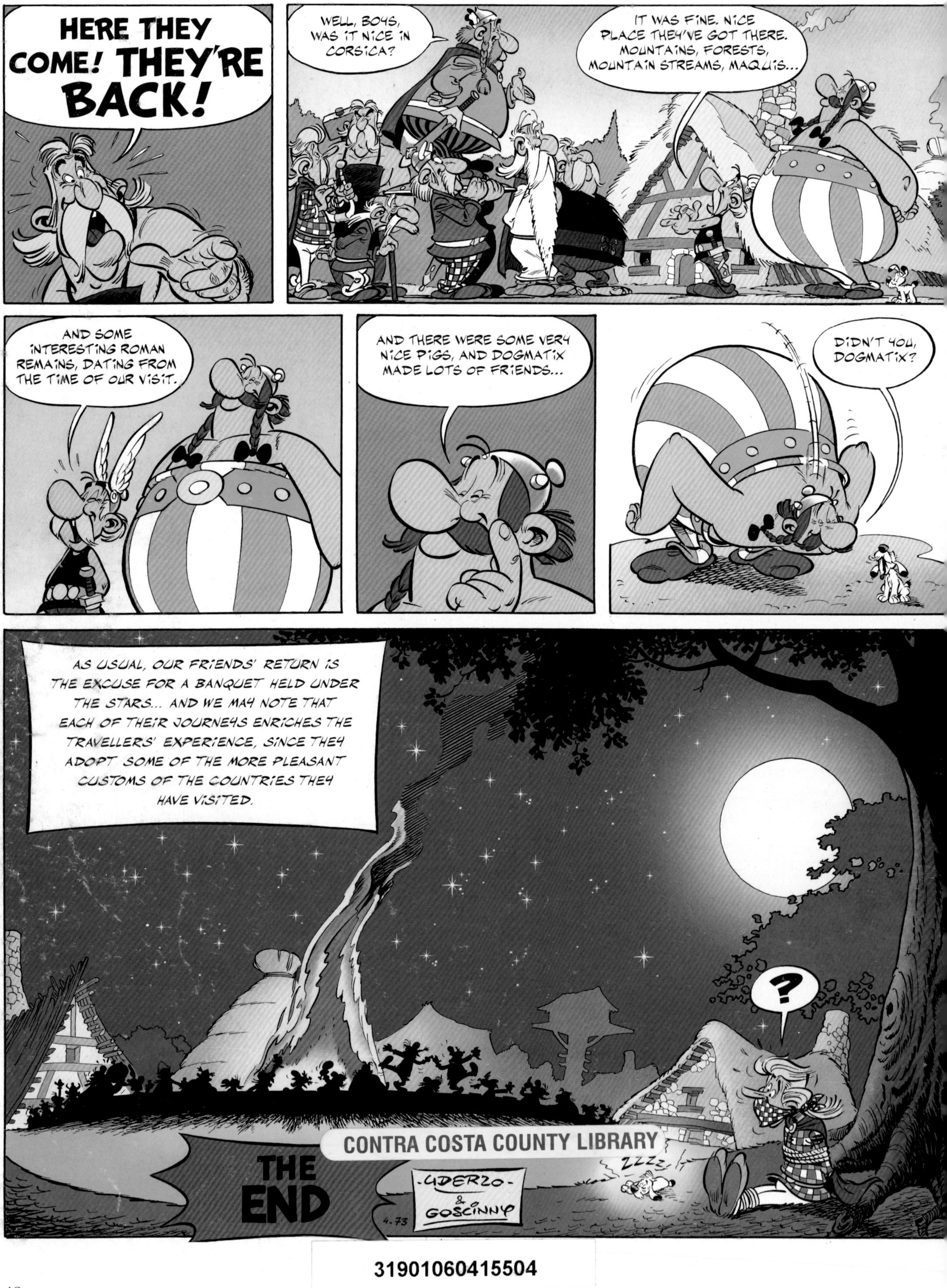
HERE THEY COME! THEY'RE BACK!
WELL, BOYS, WAS IT NICE IN CORSICA?
IT WAS FINE. NICE PLACE THEY'VE GOT THERE. MOUNTAINS, FORESTS, MOUNTAIN STREAMS, MAQUIS...
AND SOME INTERESTING ROMAN REMAINS, DATING FROM THE TIME OF OUR VISIT.
AND THERE WERE SOME VERY NICE PIGS, AND DOGMATIX MADE LOTS OF FRIENDS...
DIDN'T YOU, DOGMATIX?
AS USUAL, OUR FRIENDS' RETURN IS THE EXCUSE FOR A BANQUET HELD UNDER THE STARS... AND WE MAY NOTE THAT EACH OF THEIR JOURNEYS ENRICHES THE TRAVELLERS' EXPERIENCE, SINCE THEY ADOPT SOME OF THE MORE PLEASANT CUSTOMS OF THE COUNTRIES THEY HAVE VISITED.
?
ZZZ
THE END
UDERZO & GOSCINNY
4.73